RALPH L. ROYS
THE BOOK OF CHILAM BALAM OF CHUMAYEL

RALPH L. ROYS
THE BOOK OF CHILAM BALAM OF CHUMAYEL

THE BOOK OF
CHILAM BALAM OF CHUMAYEL
BY RALPH L. ROYS

CONTENTS

PREFACE

Among the various avenues of approach to the investigation of Maya civilization, the study of the native literature of Yucatan is, next to the actual archæological exploration of the remains, one of the most promising, for it contains much of what the Indians remembered of their old culture after the Spanish Conquest. The Books of Chilam Balam form the most important part of this native Maya literature. Written in the Maya language, they reflect more closely the thought of these Indians than any other records that have come down to us. Not only do they contain a wealth of historical and ethnological information invaluable to the student of the pre-Columbian career of the Maya, but they also furnish a record of the reactions of the native mind to the European culture and of the manner in which the latter was adapted to suit its new environment. It is hardly necessary to dwell upon the value of these old texts to the linguistic student. The translation of the Book of Chilam Balam of Chumayel depends primarily upon the reading given to the badly punctuated and often misspelled Maya text, and such a reading is based upon an extensive comparison with other similar texts. The difficulties of translation are not to be underestimated, but they can be greatly lessened by such a comparison. That I have been able to avail myself of the assistance afforded by the manuscripts of the Berendt Linguistic Collection, so often referred to in these pages, is due to the collaboration of the Museum of the University of Pennsylvania and to the kindness of Dr. Horace H. F. Jayne, Director, who has supplied me with the necessary photostats. Professor Alfred M. Tozzer, whose previous extensive survey of Maya literature was the indispensable preliminary to the present work, has given cordial assistance; both he and the Peabody Museum of American Archæology and Ethnology have cooperated generously with the loan of material necessary to the work. Mr. Frans Blom, Director, and the Department of Middle American Research of the Tulane University of Louisiana have kindly loaned photographs of Sixteenth Century Maya documents in their collection, which have proved most valuable in the study of the present text.

Dr. Sylvanus G. Morley has spent much time and thought in going over my manuscript and has offered many valuable suggestions as well as searching out and obtaining related material in Mexico and Yucatan. Mr. Thomas R. Johnson has undertaken the tedious task of copying the drawings in the Chumayel manuscript. Mr. Juan Martínez Hernández has again, as in the past, come to my aid in the elucidation of obscure phrases and badly written passages in the Maya text. Linguistic data furnished by Dr. Manuel J. Andrade and ethnological analogies suggested by Dr. Robert Redfield will be found acknowledged elsewhere in this book. The manner of editing the Maya text is that suggested by Professor Otis J. Todd, who has assisted me in adapting the methods of classical scholars to this newer field of endeavor. For a number of the text-figures, Alice P. Roys has made copies from photographs and other reproductions. To Librarian John Ridington and Assistant Librarian Dorothy Jefferd, I am indebted for the many facilities afforded by the Library of the University of British Columbia. Throughout the preparation of this work, Dr. Alfred V. Kidder has given generously of his time and attention to the practical problems involved in the task. To all these I wish to make grateful acknowledgment at this time.

RALPH L. ROYS March 30, 1932

I

(THE RITUAL OF THE FOUR WORLD-QUARTERS)

the first man of the Canul family. The white *guaje*, the *ixculun* and the gumbo-limbo are his little hut,
... The logwood tree is the hut of Yaxum, the first of the men of the Cauich family.

The lord of the people of the south is the first of the men of the Noh family. Ix-Kan-tacay is the name of the first of the men of the Puch family. They guard nine rivers; they guard nine mountains

The red flint stone is the stone of the red Mucencab. The red ceiba tree of abundance is his arbor which is set in the east. The red bullet-tree is their tree. The red zapote . . . The red-vine . . . Reddish are their yellow turkeys. Red toasted corn is their corn.

The white flint stone is their stone in the north. The white ceiba tree of abundance is the arbor of the white Mucencab. White-breasted are their turkeys. White Lima-beans are their Lima-beans. White corn is their corn.

The black flint stone is their stone in the west. The black ceiba tree of abundance is their arbor. Black speckled corn is their corn. Black tipped camotes are their camotes. Black wild pigeons are their

I

turkeys. Black *akab-chan* is their green corn. Black beans are their beans. Black Lima-beans are their Lima-beans.

The yellow flint stone is the stone of the south. The ceiba tree of abundance, the yellow ceiba tree of abundance, is their arbor. The yellow bullet-tree is their tree. Colored like the yellow bullet-tree are their camotes. Colored like the yellow bullet-tree are the wild pigeons which are their turkeys. Yellow green corn is their green corn. Yellow-backed are their beans . . .

11 Ahau was the katun when they carried burdens on their backs. Then the land-surveyor first came; this was Ah Ppizte who measured the leagues. Then there came the *chacté* shrub for marking the leagues with their walking sticks. Then he came to Uac-hab-nal} to pull the weeds along the leagues, when Mizcit Ahau came to sweep clean the leagues, when the land-surveyor came. These were long leagues that he measured.

Then a spokesman was established at the head of the mat.

Ix Noh Uc presides to the east. Ox Tocoy-moo presides to the east. Ox Pauah Ek presides to the east. Ah Miz presides to the east.

Batun presides to the north. Ah Puch presides to the north. Balam-na presides to the north. Ake presides to the north.

Iban presides to the west. Ah Chab presides to the west. Ah Tucuch preside to the west.

Ah Yamas presides to the south. Ah Puch presides to the south. Cauich presides to the south. Ah Couoh presides to the south. Ah Puc presides to the south.

The red wild bees are in the east. A large red blossom is their cup. The red Plumeria is their flower.

The white wild bees are in the north. The white pach¢a is their flower. A large white blossom is their cup. The black wild bees are in the west. The black laurel flower is their flower. A large black blossom is their cup. The yellow wild bees are in the south. A large yellow blossom is their cup . . . is their flower. Then they swarmed at ¢ecuzamil in great numbers among the magueys of the land, the calabash trees of the land, the ceiba trees of the land and the *chulul* trees of the land. Kin Pauahtun was their priest. He commanded the numerous army which guarded Ah Hulneb at Tantun in Cozumel, also Ah Yax-ac, Chinab, and Kinich Kakmo.

II.

(THE RISE OF HUNAC CEEL TO POWER)

Ah Itzimthul Chac was their commander at Ichcanzihoo. Uayom-chich was their priest at Ichcanzihoo. Canul occupied the jaguar-mat. The second Priest Chable was their ruler. Cabal Xiu was their priest. Uxmal Chac was their commander; formerly he was their priest.

Then Hapay Can was brought to Chemchan. He was pierced by an arrow when he arrived at the bloody wall there at Uxmal.

Then Chac-xib-chac was despoiled of his insignia. Zac-xib-chac and Ek

Yuuan Chac were also despoiled of their insignia. Ix Zacbeliz was the name of the maternal grandmother of the Chacs. Ek Yuuan Chac was their father. Hun Yuuan Chac was their youngest brother; Uooh-puc was his name. There was a glyph (*uooh*) written on the palm of his hand. Then a glyph was written below his throat, was also written on the sole of his foot and written within the ball of the thumb of Ah Uooh-puc. The Chacs were not gods. The only true God is our Lord Dios; they worshipped him according to the word and the wisdom of Mayapan.

Ah Kin Coba was their priest there in the fortress of Mayapan . Zulim Chan was at the west gate . Nauat was the guardian of thesouth gate. Couoh was the guardian of the east gate. Ah Ek was his companion. This was their ruler: Ah Tapay Nok Cauich was the name of their head-chief; Hunac Ceel was the representative of Ah Mex Cuc. Then he demanded one complete Plumeria flower. Then he demanded a white mat. Then he demanded a mantle faced on two sides. Then he demanded a green turkey. Then he demanded a mottled snail. Then he demanded the gourds called *homa*.

Whereupon they departed and arrived at Ppoole, where the remainder of the Itzá were increased in number; they took the women of Ppole as their mothers. Then they arrived at Ake; there they were born at Ake. Ake it was called here, as they said. Then they arrived at Alaa; Alaa was its name here, they said. Then they came to Tixchel, where their words and discourse were prolonged. Then they arrived at Ninum, where their words and conversations were many. Then they arrived at Chikin-¢onot, where their faces were turned to the west. Chikin-¢onot was its name here, so they said. Then they arrived at Tzuc-oop, where they remained apart under the Anona tree. Tzuc-op was its name here, so they said. Then they arrived at Tah-cab (Tahcabo), where the Itzas stirred the honey. Then it was drunk by X-koh-takin.

When the honey was stirred, she drank it at Cabilneba, as it was called. Then they arrived at Kikil, where they contracted dysentery. Kikil was its name here, so they said. Then they arrived at Panabhaa, where they dug for water. Then they came to Cucuchilhaa; they settled at the deep water. Then they arrived at Yalzihon; Yalzihon was its name here, where they settled the town. Then they arrived at Xppitah (Espita), also a town. Then they arrived at

Kancab¢onot. They departed and arrived at ¢ula. Then they came to Pibhaal¢onot. Then they arrived at Tahaac, as it was called. Then they came to Ticooh, where they haggled for that which was dear. Ticoh was its name here. Then they arrived at Tikal, where they shut themselves in. Tikal was its name here. Then they came to Timaax, where they made complete rogues of themselves. Then they arrived at Buctzotz, where they covered the hair of their heads with a garment. Buctzotz was its name here, so they said. Then they arrived at ¢i¢ontun, where a malevolent man began to seize the land. It was called ¢iholtun here. Then they arrived at Yobain, where the crocodile bewitched them through their maternal grandfather, Ah Yamazi, their ruler at the seashore. Then they arrived at Zinanche, where the devil bewitched them. Zinanche was its name here. Then they arrived at the town of Chac. Then they arrived at ¢euc; their companions contended with one another. Then the maternal grandfather of their companions arrived to reconcile them at ¢emul, as it was called here. Then they arrived at Kini at the home of Xkil Itzam Pech. Their companions were at X¢euc when they arrived at the home of Xkil Itzam Pech, the ruler of the people of Kini. Then they arrived at Baca, where water was poured out for them. It was Baca here, so they said. Then they arrived at Zabacnail, the home of their maternal grandfather, the first of the men of the Na family ; this was Chel Na, their maternal grandfather. Then they arrived at Tebenaa, where they remembered their mother. Then they went to Ixil. Then they went to Chulul. Then they went to Holtun-chable. Then they came to Itzamna (Itzimná). Then they came to Chubulna. Then they arrived at Caucel, where they all shivered with cold. It was Caucel here, so they said. Then they arrived at Ucu, where they said: "*ya ucu.*" Then they went to Hunucma. Then they arrived at Kinchil. Then they went to Can kana. Then they arrived at Tixpetoncah. Then they arrived at Zahab-balam. Then they arrived at Tahcum-chakan. Then they arrived at Tixbalche. Then they arrived at Uxmal. Then they departed and arrived at Tixyubak. Then they arrived at Munaa, where their words were soft. Then they went to Oxlochhok. Then they went to Chac-akal. Then they went to Xocneceh; the deer was their familiar spirit when they arrived. Then they went to Ppuztunich. Then they went to Pucnalchac. Then they went to Ppencuyut. Then they went to Paxueuet. Then they arrived at Tixaya (Xaya). Then they arrived at Tiztiz, as it is called. Then they arrived at Chican. Then they arrived at Tixmeuac.

Then they arrived at Hunacthi. Then they arrived at Titzal. Then they arrived at Tamuzbulna. Then they arrived at Tixcan. Then they arrived at Lop. Then they arrived at Cheemiuan. Then they arrived at Oxcauanka. Then they went to Zacbacelcan. Then they arrived at Cetelac.

These are the names of whatever towns there were and the names of the wells, in order that it may be known where they passed in their march to see whether this district was good, whether it was suitable for settlement here. They set in order the names of the district according to the command of our Lord God. He it was who set the land in order. He created everything on earth. He set it in order also. But these were the people who named the district, who named the wells, who named the villages, who named the land because no one had arrived here in this neck of the land when we arrived here.

Zubinche, Kaua, Cumcanul (Cuncunul), Tiemtun (Ebtun), where the precious stones descended, Zizal, Zacii (Valladolid), Ti¢ooc (Tesoco), where the law of the katun was fulfilled, Timozon, Popola, where the mat of the katun was spread, Tipixoy (Pixoy), Uayumhaa (Uayma), Zacbacelean, Tinum where little was said to them, Timacal, Popola where they counted the mat of the katun in its order, Tixmaculum where they interrupted with words, ¢ithaaz (¢itas), Bon-kauil, Tixmex, Kochila, Tixxocen (Xocen), Chunpak, Pibahul, Tunkaaz (Tunkas), Haltunhaa, Kuxbila, ¢i¢ilche, Zitilpech, Chalamte where their anger was appeased, Itzamthulil (Izamal), Tipakab (Tepakam?) where they were united,

Tiya (Teya), Caanzahcab, ¢i¢omtun, together with their maternal grandfather . . . ¢i¢holtun, Popola to the south of Zinanche. Then they came to Muci, Zacnicte-cheen, Zo¢il; here they had a council of war at Multumut, as it was called here, Mutul. Muxuppipp, Ake, Hoctun, where they settled at the base of the stone, Xoc-chel, Bohe, Zahcabhaa (Sancaba?), Tzanlahcat (Sanahcat), Human where there were noisy talk and rumors about them. Chalamte, Pacaxua was its name here they said. Tekit where the remainder of the Itzá were dispersed, Yokolcheen, Ppuuppulni-huh (Huhi?) the iguana was their familiar spirit when they came forth. ¢o¢il, Tiab (Teabo), Bitun-cheen. Then they entered Tipikal, as the well was called, after which they came up out of it. Then they went to Poc-huh, as the well was named, where they roasted the iguana. Then they went to Mani, where their language was forgotten by them. Then they arrived at Ti¢aan (¢am); three days they were submerged. Then they went to Ticul, Zacluum-cheen (Sacalum), Tixtohil-cheen (Xtohil), where they recovered their health. Then they went to Balam-kin, the district of the priests. Cheenchomac, Zacnicteel¢onot (Sacnicte), Tiyaxcab (Yaxcaba?), Uman, Oxcum, Zanhil (Samahil), Ichcanzihoo (Mérida), Ti-noh-naa, Nohpat, Poychena, Chulul (Cholul). Then they arrived at the corner of the land, Cumkal (Conkal), where the corner of the district was set. Zicpach, Yaxkukul,

Tixkokob, Cuca, Cheen-balam, Bolon-nic-xan, Ekol, Ekol was the name of the well here. Tixueue, Tixueue was the name of the well here. Uhumtal, where one part came. Tixkanimacal, Tixaan (Texan), Yumxul, where they took their father-in-law as their lord. Holtun-ake (Ake?), Acanceh, Ticooh (Tecoh), Tichahil, Tichac (Telchaquillo?), Mayapan the fortress, Yokol-haa. Then they went to Nabula, Tixmucuy (Timucuy), Tixkanhube, ¢oyila (¢oyola). Then they arrived at Tizip, where their words and conversation were sinful.

Then the rulers began to establish the country. There was the priest at Paloncab; there was the priest at Mutupul (Mutul), as it was called. The priest at Paloncab was Ah May; The priest at Mutul was Ah Canul, also entitled Uayom Chich, who spoke brokenly also; also the second Chable man, the man of Ichcanziho, Holtun Balam, his son. Then the province of Chakan received the quetzal. Then their associate rulers arrived. These rulers were the intimate associates of the rulers in Tun 11 Ahau. Then they established the land; then they established the country. Then they settled at Ichcanziho. Then came the people of Holtun-Ake; then came the people of Zabacna. Then the rulers came, all together. The man of Zabacna was the first of the men of the Na family. Then they assembled at Ichcanziho, where the official mat was, during the reign of Holtun

Balam, there at the well, during the reign of Pochek-ix-¢oy. He was the first of the men of Copo; Tutul Xiu might have been there also. Chacte was the ruler, Chacte was the land where their rulers arrived. Teppanciz was their priest, he was looked upon as such. It was Ah Ppizte who measured their land. But Lubte was the land where they rested, there were seven leagues of land. Ah May it was who fixed the corners of the land, he who set the corners in their places; the sweeper who swept the land was Mizcit Ahau. But the land which was established for them was Hoyahelcab; there they came to the use of their reason. They proved their ruler, they proved their reason.

Then began the introduction of tribute to them at Chichen. At Tikuch arrived the tribute of the four men. 11 Ahau was the name of the katun when the tribute was handled. There at Cetelac it was assembled; there it was. Then came the tribute of Holtun Zuiua, there at Cetelac, where they agreed in their opinions. 13 Ahau was the name of the katun when the head-chiefs received the tribute.

Then began their reign; then began their rule. Then they began to be served; then those who were to be thrown (into the cenote) arrived; then they began to throw them into the well that their prophecy might be heard by their rulers. Their prophecy did not come. It was Cauich, Hunac Ceel, Cauich was the name of the man there, who put out his head at the opening of the well on the south side. Then he went to take it. Then he came forth to declare the prophecy. Then began the taking of the prophecy. Then began his prophecy. Then they began to declare him ruler. Then he was set in the seat of the rulers by them. Then they began to declare him head-chief. He was not the ruler formerly; that was only the office of Ah Mex Cuc. Now the representative of Ah Mex Cuc was declared ruler. The eagle, they say, was his mother. Then, they say, he was sought on his hill. Then they began to take the prophecy of this ruler after it was declared. Then they began to set aloft the house on high for the ruler. Then began the construction of the stairway. Then he was set in the house on high in 13 Ahau, the sixth reign. Then began the hearing of the prophecy, of the news, of the setting up of Ah Mex Cuc, as he was called. Then he carried nearly to Baca the news of Ah Mex Cuc. He was placed there. Then he began to be treated as a lord; then obedience to the name of Ah Mex Cuc began. Then he was obeyed; then he was served there at the mouth of the well. Chichen Itzam was its name because the Itza went there. Then he removed the stones of the land, the stones of the sowed land, the place of Itzam, and they went into the water. Then began the introduction of misery there at Chichen Itzá. Then he went to the east and arrived at the home of Ah Kin Coba.

Katun 8 Ahau came. 8 Ahau was the name of the katun when their government occurred. Then there was a change of the katun, then there was a change of rulers.

. . . when our rulers increased in numbers, according to the words of their priest to them. Then they introduced the drought. That which came was a drought, according to their words, when the hoofs of the animals burned, when the seashore burned, a sea of misery. So it was said on high, so it was said. Then the face of the sun was eaten; then the face of the sun was darkened; then its face was extinguished. They were terrified on high, when it burned at the word of their priest to them, when the word of our ruler was fulfilled at the word of their priest to them. Then began the idea of painting the exterior of the sun. When they heard of that, they saw the moon. Then came the rulers of the land. It was Ix-Tziu-nene who introduced sin to us, the slaves of the land, when he came. Then the law of the katun, the divination of the katun shall be fulfilled. When he was brought, what was your command, you, the rulers of the land? Then the law of another katun was introduced, at the end of the katun when Ix-Tziu-nene was brought. Whereupon a numerous army was seen, and they began to be killed. Then a thing of terror was constructed, a gallows for their death. Now began the archery of Ox-halal Chan. Then the rulers of the land were called. Their blood flowed, and it was taken by the archers. They were terrified . . . the time when the katun ended for them . . .

III

(A PROPHECY FOR KATUN 11 AHAU)

Katun 11 Ahau is set upon the mat, set upon the throne, when their ruler is set up. Yaxal Chac is its face to their ruler. The heavenly fan, the heavenly wreath and the heavenly bouquet shall descend. The drum and rattle of the lord of 11 Ahau shall resound, when flint knives are set into his mantle. At that time there shall be the green turkey; at that time there shall be Zulim Chan; at that time there shall be Chakanputun. They shall find their food among the trees; they shall find their food among the rocks, those who have lost their usual food in katun 11 Ahau.

11 Ahau is the beginning of the count, because this was the katun when the foreigners arrived. They came from the east when they arrived. Then

Christianity also began. The fulfilment of its prophecy is ascribed to the east. The katun is established at Ichcaanzihoo.

This is a record of the things which they did. After it had all passed, they told of it in their own words, but its meaning is not plain. Still the course of events was as it is written. But even when everything shall be thoroughly explained, perhaps not so much is written about it, nor has very much been written of the guilt of their conspiracies with one another. So it was with the ruler of the Itzá, with the men who were rulers of Izamal, Ake, Uxmal, Ichcanziho and Citab Couoh also. Very many were the head-chiefs and many a conspiracy they made with one another. But they are not made known in what is written here; not so much will be related. Still he who comes of our lineage will know it, one of us who are Maya men. He will know how to explain these things when he reads what is here. When he sees it, then he will explain the adjustment of the intricacy of the katun by our priest, Ah Kin Xuluc; but Xuluc was not his name formerly. It was only because these priests of ours were to come to an end when misery was introduced, when Christianity was introduced by the real Christians. Then with the true God, the true *Dios*, came the beginning of our misery. It was the beginning of tribute, the beginning of church dues, the beginning of strife with purse-snatching, the beginning of strife with blow-guns, the beginning of strife by trampling on people, the beginning of robbery with violence, the beginning of forced debts, the beginning of debts enforced by false testimony, the beginning of individual strife, a beginning of vexation, a beginning of robbery with violence. This was the origin of service to the Spaniards and priests, of service to the local chiefs, of service to the teachers, of service to the public prosecutors by the boys, the youths of the town, while the poor people were harassed. These were the very poor people who did not depart when oppression was put upon them. It was by Antichrist on earth, the kinkajous of the towns, the foxes of the towns, the blood-sucking insects of the town, those who drained the poverty of the working people. But it shall still come to pass that tears shall come to the eyes of our Lord God. The justice of our Lord God shall descend upon every part of the world, straight from God upon Ah Kantenal, Ix Pucyola, the avaricious hagglers of the world.

IV

(THE BUILDING OF THE MOUNDS)

In the year 1541.

181 ȼuul. at. 5 Dik: 92 nhele

The history which I have written of how the mounds came to be constructed by the heathen. During three score and fifteen katuns they were constructed. The great men made them. Then the remainder of the men went to Cartabona, as the land where they were is called today. There they were when San Bernabé came to teach them. Then they were killed by the men; the men were called heathen. 1 5 56 is the total count today after fifteen years. On this day I have written how the great mounds came to be built by the lineages and all the things which the rulers did. They were the ones who built the mounds. It took thirteen katuns and six years for them to construct them. The following was the beginning of the mounds they built. Fifteen four-hundreds were the scores of their mounds, and fifty more made the total count of the mounds they constructed all over the land. From the sea to the base of the land they created names for them as well as for the wells. Then a miracle was performed for them by God. Then they were burned by fire among the people of Israel. This is the record of the katuns and years since Chac-unezcab of the lineage of the Tutul Xius departed from Viroa.

V

(MEMORANDA CONCERNING THE HISTORY OF YUCATAN)

A record of the katuns and years when the Province of Yucatan was first seized by the foreigners, the white men. It was, they say, in Katun 11 Ahau that they seized the port of Ecab. They came from the east when they arrived. They say they were the first to eat the pond-apple for breakfast, this was the reason they called them the foreigners who ate pond-apples; foreigners who sucked pond-apples, they were called. This is the name of the householder whom they seized at Ecab, Nacom Balam was his name. He was the first to be seized at Ecab by the first Spanish captain, Don Juan de Montejo, the first conqueror. It was still the same katun when they arrived at Ichcanziho (Merida).

It was the year 1513 in Katun 13 Ahau that they seized Campeche. They were there one katun. Ah Kin Camal from Campeche introduced the foreigners into the province here.

It was on August 20th in the year 1541, I have made known the name of the year when Christianity began.

In the year 1519, after seven score and eleven years, occurred the agreement with the foreigners, according to which we paid for the war between the foreigners and the other men here in the towns. It was the captains of the towns who made war . It is we who pay for it today.

Today I have written down that in the year 1541 the foreigners first arrived from the east at Ecab, as it was called. In that year occurred their arrival at the port of Ecab, at the village of Nacom Balam, on the first day of the year in which Katun 11 Ahau fell . After the Itzá were dispersed, it was fifteen score years when the foreigners arrived. It was after the town of Zaclahtun was depopulated, after the town of Kinchil Coba was depopulated, after the town of Chichen Itzá was depopulated, after the town on the Uxmal side of the range of hills , the great town of Uxmal as it is called, was depopulated, as well as Kabah. It was after the towns of Zeye, Pakam, Homtun, at the town of Tix-calom-kin, and Ake, Holtun Ake, were depopulated.

It was after the town of Emal Chac was depopulated, Izamal, where the daughter of the true God, Lord of Heaven, descended, the Queen, the Virgin, the miraculous One. When the ruler said: "The shield of Kinich Kakmo shall descend," he was not declared ruler here. It was she, the miraculous one, the merciful one, who was so declared here. "The rope shall descend, the cord shall descend from heaven. The word shall descend from heaven." There was rejoicing over his reign by the other towns when they said this, but he was not declared their ruler at Emal (Izamal?).

Then the great Itzá went away . Thirteen four-hundreds were the four-hundreds of their thousands, and fifteen four-hundreds, the four-hundreds of their hundreds, the leading men among them, the heathen Itzá. But many supporters went with them to feed them. Thirteen measures of corn per head was their quota, and nine measures and three handsful of grain. From many small towns the magicians went with them also.

They did not wish to join with the foreigners; they did not desire Christianity. They did not wish to pay tribute, did those whose emblems were the bird, the precious stone, the flat precious stone and the jaguar, those with the three magic emblems . Four four-hundreds of years and fifteen score years was the end of their lives; then came the end of their lives, because they knew the measure of their days. Complete was the month; complete, the year; complete, the day; complete, the night; complete, the breath of life as it passed also; complete, the blood, when they arrived at their beds, their mats, their thrones. In due measure did they recite the good prayers; in due measure they sought the lucky days, until they saw the good stars enter into their reign; then they kept watch while the reign of the good stars began. Then everything was good.

Then they adhered to the dictates of their reason. There was no sin; in the holy faith their lives were passed . There was then no sickness; they had then no aching bones; they had then no high fever; they had then no smallpox; they had then no burning chest; they had then no abdominal pains; they had then no consumption; they had then no headache. At that time the course of humanity was orderly. The foreigners made it otherwise when they arrived here. They brought shameful things when they came. They lost their innocence in carnal sin; they lost their innocence in the carnal sin of Nacxit Xuchit, in the carnal sin of his companions. No lucky days were then displayed to us. This was the origin of the two-day chair (or throne), of the two-day reign; this was the cause of our sickness also. There were no more lucky days for us; we had no sound judgment. At the end of our loss of vision, and of our shame, everything shall be revealed. There was no great teacher, no great speaker, no supreme priest, when the change of rulers occurred at their arrival. Lewd were the priests, when they came to be established here by the foreigners. Furthermore they left their descendants here at Tancah (Mayapan). These then received the misfortunes, after the affliction of these foreigners. These, they say, were the Itzá. Three times it was, they say, that the foreigners arrived. It was because of this that we were relieved from paying tribute at the age of sixty, because of the affliction by these men, the Itzá. It was not we who did it; it is we who pay for it today. However there is at last an agreement so that there may be peace between us and the foreigners. Otherwise there will be a great war.

VI

(NOTES ON THE CALENDAR)

The beginning of Katun 11 Ahau was in the year	1513
Then it ended.	
Tihoo (Merida) was begun in the year	1519
(The convent of) San Francisco was founded at Santiago in Tihoo	1519
The principal church was founded in the center of the town of Ti hoo in the year	1540
The months in a year are twelve	12
The count of the days in one year	365
The count of the nights in one year	365
The count of weeks in one year	52
The number of Sundays in one year	53
The count of the days in the first six months (of the year)	181

The count of days in the second six months which complete the year   184

This is the count of days in a week: seven days in one week is the total of this count.

The count of the uinals in one year.

Poop--July 16th.

Yaax--January 12th.
The time is good for gathering the ears of corn.

Uoo--August 5th.

Zac.--
February 1st, when the white flowers bloom.

Zip-August 25th.

Ceeh--February 21st.

Zoȼ--September 14th.

Mac--March 13th when the turtles lay their eggs.

Zec--October 4th.

Kankin-- April 2d.

Xul--October 24th, when the fish spawn.

Muan--April 22nd, when there is a ring around the sun in the sky.

Çeyaxkin -- November 13th. The corn-stalks are bent double.

Paax--May 12th.

Mol--December 3rd.

Kayab--June 1st.

December 23rd.

Cheen--

Cumku--June 21st. The five days called Uayabhaab.

Chumayel, 28, is born the god-daughter, Micaela Castañeda

VII

THE ARMORIAL BEARINGS OF YUCATAN

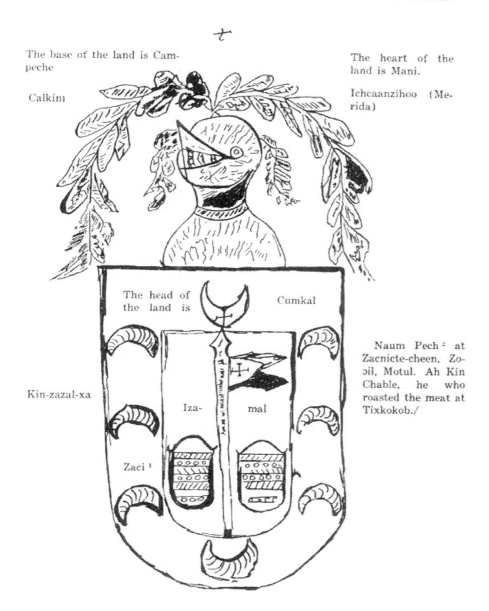

The base of the land is Campeche

Calkini

The heart of the land is Mani.

Ichcaanzihoo (Merida)

The head of the land is

Cumkal

Kin-zazal-xa

Iza-

mal

Zaci[1]

Naum Pech[2] at Zacnicte-cheen, Zooil, Motul. Ah Kin Chable, he who roasted the meat at Tixkokob./

VIII

(NOTES ON ASTRONOMY)

(Small picture of a cross.)

When the eleventh day of June shall come, it will be the longest day. When the thirteenth day of September comes, this day and night are precisely the same in length . When the twelfth day of December shall come the day

is short, but the night begins to shorten. When the tenth day of March comes, the day and night will be equal in length.

This annulus in the center of the disk is white and indicates the course of the sun. Between the two rings the black spots indicate the face of the sun, which goes over the large black one and descends to the small black one. Thus its movement is uniform, and this is its course here on earth also. On the ground it is thus manifested plainly all over the earth also. The progress of the sun is truly great as it takes its course to enter into the great *Oro* extended over the world. This is the record of the motion of the sun as it is known here on earth.

To the people on the sides of this half-section as pictured, the sun is not eclipsed; but for anyone who is in the middle it is eclipsed. It is in conjunction with the moon when it is eclipsed. It travels in its course before it is eclipsed. It arrives in its course to the north, very great. It is all the same with eclipses of the sun and moon before it arrives opposite to the sun. This is the explanation so that Maya people may know what happens to the sun and to the Moon.

IX

(THE INTERROGATION OF THE CHIEFS)

This is the language of Zuyua and the understanding for our lord, Señor Governor Mariscal, who has settled at Tzuc-uaxim to the east of Ichcanziho (Merida). This is the land where his garden and homestead were, where he settled. Then the day will come when his period of office shall end also. The command of the head-chief comes. Vigorous is his command, when he arrives, and red is his garment also.

On this day, in the language of Zuyua, this is the question asked by the head-chief of the town; then the day shall arrive when the law of Katun 3 Ahau shall end, when another katun shall be set in its place , Katun 1 Ahau, as stated below.

This katun today is Katun 3 Ahau. The time has come for the end of its rule and reign. It is finished. Another one takes its place for a time.

This is Katun 1 Ahau, which is set within the house of Katun 3 Ahau. There it is its guest, while it is given its power by Katun 3 Ahau. Things are shameful, they say, in the place where they dwell.

This is the examination which takes place in the katun which ends today. The time has arrived for examining the knowledge of the chiefs of the towns, to see whether they know how the ruling men came, whether they have explained the coming of the chiefs, of the head-chiefs, whether they are of the lineage of rulers, whether they are of the lineage of chiefs, that they may prove it.

This is the first question which will be asked of them: he shall ask them for his food "Bring the sun." This is the word of the head-chief to them; thus it is said to the chiefs. "Bring the sun, my son, bear it on the palm of your hand to my plate. A lance is planted, a lofty cross, in the middle of its heart. A green jaguar is seated over the sun to drink its blood." Of Zuyua is the wisdom. This is what the sun is which is demanded of them: a very large fried egg. This is the lance and the lofty cross planted in its heart of which he speaks: it is the benediction. This is what the green jaguar is which is set over it to drink its blood: it is a green chile-pepper, is the jaguar. This is the language of Zuyua.

This is the second question that will be asked of them: let them go and get the brains of the sky, so the head-chief may see how large they are. "It is my desire to see them; let me see them." This is what he would say to them. This is what the brains of the sky are: it is copal gum. Zuyua language .

This is the third question which will be asked of them: let them construct a large house. Six *thils* is its length., one such measure is that of its upright timbers. This is what the large house is: it is a very large hat set on the floor. He shall be told to mount a very large white horse. White shall be his mantle and his cape, and he shall grasp a white rattle in his hand, while he rattles it at his horse. There is coagulated blood on the rosette of his rattle, which comes out of it. This is what the white horse is: it is a stirrup of henequen fiber. This is the white rattle mentioned, and the white cape: they are a Plumeria flower and a white wreath. This is the coagulated blood on the rosette of the rattle, which is demanded of them: it is the gold in the middle, because it is blood which comes from the veins of the fatherless and motherless orphan.

This is the fourth question which will be asked of them: Let them go to his house and then they shall be told: "When you come, you shall be visible at midday. You shall be children again, you shall creep again . When you arrive, your little dog shall be just behind you. This little dog of yours carries with its teeth the soul of our holy mistress, when you come with it." This is what the second childhood at midday is, which is mentioned to him. He shall go where he casts a shadow, this is what is called creeping. Then he shall come to the house of the head-chief. This is what his little dog is which is demanded of him: it is his wife. This is what the soul of our holy mistress is: it is an enormous thick wax candle. This is the language of Zuyua.

This is the fifth question which will be asked of them. They shall be told to go and get the heart of God the Father in heaven. "Then you shall bring me thirteen layers wrapped up in a coarse white fabric." This is the heart of God the Father, of which they are told: it is a bead of precious stone. This is what the covering of thirteen layers is, which is mentioned. It is an enormous tortilla. Thirteen layers of beans are in it. This is what the coarse white fabric is, it is a white mantle. This shall be demanded of them, as signified in the language of Zuyua.

This is the sixth question which will be asked of them: to go and get the branch of the *pochote* tree, and a cord of three strands, and a living liana. This he will relish. "My food for tomorrow. It is my desire to eat it." It is not bad to gnaw the trunk of the *pochote* tree, so they are told. This is what the trunk of the *pochote* tree is: it is a lizard. This is the cord of three strands, the tail of an iguana. This is the living liana, it is the entrails of a pig. This is the trunk of the *pochote* tree, the base of the tail of a lizard. The language of Zuyua.

This is the seventh question which will be asked of them. They shall be told: "Go and gather for me those things which plug the bottom of the cenote, two white ones, two yellow ones. I desire to eat them." These are the things which plug the bottom of the cenote, which are demanded of them. They are two white and two yellow jícamas. These are the things to be understood in order to become chiefs of the town, when they are brought before the ruler, the first head-chief.

These are the words. If they are not understood by the chiefs of the towns, ill-omened is the star adorning the night. Frightful is its house. Sad is the havoc in the courtyards of the nobles. Those who die are those who do not understand; those who live will understand it. This competitive test shall hang over the

27

chiefs of the towns; it has been copied so that the severity may be known in which the reign is to end. Their hands are bound before them to a wooden collar. They are pulled along with the cord. They are taken to the house of the ruler, the first head-chief. This is the end of the chiefs. This shall hang over the unrestrained lewd ones of the day and of the katun. They shall feel anguish when the affairs of the chiefs of the towns shall come to an end. This shall occur on the day when the law of the katun shall come to an end, when Katun 3 Ahau shall terminate. The chiefs of the towns shall be seized because they are lacking in understanding.

Thus shall occur the seizure of the chiefs of the towns. This is the memorandum so that they may give the first head-chief his food, when he demands his food of them. They shall be hung by the neck; the tips of their tongues shall be cut off: their eyes shall be torn out. On this day the end shall come.

But those who are of the lineage shall come forth before their lord on bended knees in order that their wisdom may be made known. Then their mat is delivered to them and their throne as well. The test is to be seen as it is copied here. Those of the lineage of the first head-chief here in the land are viewed with favor. They shall live on that day, and they shall also receive their first wand of office. Thus are those of the lineage of Maya men established again in the Province of Yucatan. God shall be first, when all things are accomplished here on earth. He is the true ruler, he shall come to demand of us our government, those things which we hold sacred, precious stones, precious beads; and he shall demand the planted wine, the *balché*. He who has none shall be killed. He who obeys, godly is his action according to the law. But perhaps God will not desire all the things which have been written to come to pass.

So, also, these are the nobility, the lineage of the chiefs, who know whence come the men and the rulers of their government. The discretion with which they govern their subjects shall be viewed with favor. Their mat and

their throne shall be delivered to them by our lord, the first head-chief. This is their mat and their throne. But the unrestrained upstart of the day and katun, the offspring of the mad woman, the offspring of the harlot, the son of evil, the two-day occupant of the mat, the two-day occupant of the throne, the rogue of the reign, the rogue of the katun, he shall be roughly handled, his face covered with earth, trampled into the ground, and befouled, as he is dragged along. On the other hand , the ruling men of noble lineage have walked abroad in Katun 3 Ahau; they are placated in the fullness of their hearts when they are told to go and take the chiefs of the towns. Then let them go and take them.

"Son, go and bring the flower of the night to me here." This is what will be said. Then let him go on his knees before the head-chief who demands this of him. "Father, here is the flower of the night for which you ask me; I come with it and with the vile thing of the night. There it is with me." These are his words.

"Then, my son, if it is with you, have you with you the first captive and the great álamo tree?" "Father, they are with me. I have come with them."

"Then, my son, if you have come with them, go and call your companions to me. These are an old man with nine sons and an old woman with nine children." "Father," he says when he replies, "I have come with them. Here they are with me. First they came to me, and then I came to see you."

"Then, my son, if they are here with you, go and gather for me stones of the savannah and come with them." He gathers them to his breast when he comes. "Are you a head-chief? Are you of the lineage of the ruler here in the land?" The language of Zuyua.

This is the flower of the night which is demanded of him: a star in the sky. This is the vile thing of the night: it is the moon. This is the first woman captive and the great álamo tree: it is the town official, named "he who falls to the ground." This is the old man with nine sons who is demanded of him: it is his great toe. This is the old woman demanded of him: it is his thumb. These are the stones of the savannah which are sought for and which his son is to gather to his breast: they are quails.

"Also, my son, where is the smooth green thing of which you were told? You were not told to look at its face." Here it is with me, father." "Then, my son, go and bring to me here the placenta of the sky.

When you come from the east, you shall come with something close behind you." "So be it, father," he says.

This is what the smooth green thing is, which is with him when he arrives: it is the rind of a squash. This is the placenta of the sky which is demanded of him: it is moulded copal-gum shaped into thirteen layers. This is what is said to come close behind him: it is the shadow at his back early in the afternoon.

" My son, you are a head-chief; you are a ruler also. Go and get me the green beads with which you pray."

These are the green beads which are demanded of him: it is a bead of precious stone. Then he shall be asked how many days he prays. "Father," he says, "for one day I pray, and for ten days I pray." "On what day does your prayer arise?" "Father, on the ninth day and on the thirteenth day. It is to Bolon-ti-ku and Oxlahun-ti-citbil that I count my beads."

" My son, go and get me your loin-cloth that I may perceive its odor here with the wide spread odor of my loin-cloth, the odor of my mantle, the odor of my censer, the supreme odor at the center of the sky, at the center of the clouds, also that which glues together my mouth, it is in a white carved cup . Do this if you are a head-chief." "Father, I will bring them," he says.

This is the odor of the loin-cloth which he asks for, this is the supreme odor at the center of the sky: it is copal gum set on fire so that it burns. This is what first glues together his mouth: it is ground cacao, chocolate.

"Then, my son, go bring me the green blood of my daughter, also her head, her entrails, her thigh, and her arm; also that which I told you to enclose in an unused jar, as well as the green stool of my daughter. Show them to me. It is my desire to see them. I have commissioned you to set them before me, that I may burst into weeping." "So be it, father." He is to come with the left ear of a wild bee. Then let him go.

This is the green blood of his daughter for which he asks: it is Maya wine. These are the entrails of his daughter: it is an empty bee-hive. This is his daughter's head: it is an unused jar for steeping wine. This is what his daughter's green stool is: it is the stone pestle for pounding honey. This is what the left ear of the wild bee is: it is a drop of the moisture of the wine. This is what the bone of his daughter is: it is the flexible bark of the balché. This is the thigh of which he speaks: it is the trunk of the *balché* tree. This is what the arm of his daughter is: it is the branch of the *balché*. This is what he calls weeping: it is a drunken speech. Then let him go and give these things to him. Let him seat himself tranquilly; let him wait for him to speak; let him salute him as his lord when he arrives.

"Father, here is your daughter whom you put in my care. of whom you speak. You are the father, you are the ruler." This is what his son says to him.

"Oh son, my fellow head-chief, my fellow ruler! You have remembered; it is sufficient. You know; it is sufficient," he says. "This, then, is the blood of my daughter for which I ask you." Thirteen times the blood of his daughter flows, while he weeps for his daughter, lying there in the courtyard. Perchance, then he weeps, while he looks at her, bowed down, while he says: "Oh son!" he says while he weeps, "you are a head-chief. Oh son, you are a ruler also. Oh my fellow head-chief, I will deliver your mat and your throne and your authority to you, son; yours is the government, yours is the authority also, my son."

Thus, then, the chiefs of the towns are to obey him when they depart with the first head-chief, there at the head of the province. Then let them go to his house. There they are at his house, when they give his food to the head-chief, and when he asks them for his food, as he shall specify in its order.

"Son, bring me four cardinals which are at the mouth of the cave. They are to be set over the first thing which glues together my mouth. It is to be red, that which I call the crest over the first thing which glues together my mouth, when it shall be brought before me." "It is well, father." What he asks for are little cakes of achiote. This is the crest of which he speaks: it is the froth on the chocolate.

This is what first glues together his mouth: it is cacao which has been ground. The language of Zuyua.

"Son, bring me the bird of the night and the drilled stone of the night, and with them the brains of the sky. Great is my desire to see them here." "It is well, father." What he wants is a stick used to scrape copal gum from the tree . This the drilled stone of the night for which he asks, a bead of precious stone. The brains of the sky are copal gum. Language of Zuyua.

"Son, bring me the bone of your father whom you buried three years ago. Great is my desire to see it." "It is well, father." This is what he wants, it is cassava baked in a pit. Then let him go and give it to the head-chief.

"Son, bring me an old man whose coat is not buttoned, Homtochac is his name." "It is well, father." What he asks for is a nine-banded armadillo, a female armadillo.

"Son, bring me three segments split from the sky. I desire to eat them." "Even so, father."

This is what he demands, it is *atole* shaken to a froth, the froth of *atole* (maize gruel). Everything is asked in the language of Zuyua.

"Son, bring me a stock of maguey, the thick stalk of the maguey without branches. Do not remove its tip. Also bring with it three strands of ravelled cord." "It is well, father." This is what he asks for, a hog's head baked in a pit. Then he shall go and give it to him. The tip of which he speaks is its tongue, because its tip is fresh and tender.

"Son, bring me the hawks of the night for me to eat." It is well, father." What he asks for are chickens, cocks.

"Son, say to the first female captive, called Otlom-cabal, to bring me a basket of blackbirds caught beneath the great álamo tree, heaped up there in the shadow of the álamo." "Even so, father." What he asks for are some black beans that are in the house of the town official, that is, the so-called first female captive and the thing which falls limply to the ground of which he speaks. Language of Zuyua.

31

"Son, go and catch the jaguar of the cave, so that by means of you it may give savour to my food. I desire to eat the jaguar." "It is well, father." This is the jaguar for which he asks, it is an agouti. The language of Zuyua.

"Son, bring me seven coverings of the fatherless orphan . It is my desire to eat them at the time when they should be eaten." "Even so, father." This is what he asks for, it is the pressed leaves of the chaya.

"Son, bring me the green gallants here. Let them come and dance, that I may look on with pleasure. Let them come with drum and rattle, fan and drum-stick. I am expecting them." "Even so, father." What he asks for is a turkey-cock.

The drum is its crop. The rattle is its head. The fan is its tail. The drum-stick is its leg. The language of Zuyua.

"Son, bring me the fanciful desire of the district. I desire to eat it." What he asks for is clarified honey. The language of Zuyua.

"Son, bring me a stone from burned over land, it is burning hot. Bring with it the liquor for me to extinguish it, so it will crack here before me." What he wants is a *macal* baked in a pit. The liquor to extinguish it is clarified honey. The language of Zuyua.

"Son, bring me the firefly of the night. Its odor shall pass to the north and to the west. Bring with it the beckoning tongue of the jaguar." "It is well, father." What he asks for is a smoking tube filled with tobacco. The beckoning tongue of the jaguar for which he asks is fire.

"Son, bring me your daughter that I may see her. Pale is her face and very beautiful. White are her head-covering and her sash. I greatly desire her." tilt is well, father." What he asks for is a white calabash cup filled with atole. The language of Zuyua.

"Son, bring me the thing called *zabel*. Fragrant is its odor." "Even so, father." This is what he asks for, it is a melon.

"Son, bring me the green curved neck, it is bright green along the back. I desire to eat it." "It is well, father." What he asks for is the neck of a turkey-cock. Language of Zuyua.

"Son, bring me a woman with a very white and well rounded calf. Here will I tuck back the skirt from her calf." "It is well, father." He wants a jícama. This is what tucking back the skirt is: it is peeling the skin.

"Son, bring me a very beautiful woman with a very white countenance. I greatly desire her. I will cast down her skirt and her loose dress before me." "It is well, father." This is what he asks for, it is a turkey-hen for him to eat. Casting down her skirt and loose dress means plucking its feathers. Then let it be roasted for eating. The language of Zuyua.

"Son, bring to me here a farmer, an old man. I wish to see his face." "Even so, father." What he asks for is a *cucut-macal* to eat. This is the questionnaire.

"Son, bring me a farmer's wife, an old woman, a dark colored person. She is seven palms across the hips. It is my desire to see her." What he wants is the green fruit of a squash-vine. The language of Zuyua.

The day shall come.

On this day our lord, the first head-chief, trampled them under foot, when he arrived here in the land, in the land of Yucalpeten. He calls the chiefs, and the chiefs shall come. They are called by our lord, the first head-chief. "Are you chieftains?" "We are, my lord." These are their words.

"Sons, if you are head-chiefs here in the land," they shall be told, "go and get the winged jaguar, and then come and give it to me to eat. Put his bead collar on him properly, put on his crest properly, and come and give him to me to eat. Go immediately today, and come soon. Sons, I greatly desire to eat him. You are my sons, you are head-chiefs." Those who are ignorant shall be sad at heart and in countenance. They shall say nothing. But those who know shall be cheerful when they go to get the winged jaguar. Then he shall come with it. "Is it you, son?" "It is I, father." "Are you of the lineage, son?" "Indeed I am, father." "Where are your companions, son?" "Father, they are in the forest seeking the jaguar." The jaguar, as they call it, does not exist, but let him bring it before him. This jaguar for which he asks is the chief's horse which he wishes to eat. It is a horse raised about the house. This is the bead collar: it is its little bells. This is its crest: it is a red thread. It is to be completely saddled and bridled. The language of Zuyua.

X

(THE CREATION OF THE WORLD)

It is most necessary to believe this. These are the precious stones which our Lord, the Father, has abandoned. This was his first repast, this *balché*, with which we, the ruling men revere him here. Very rightly they worshipped as true gods these precious stones, when the true God was established, our Lord God, the Lord of heaven and earth, the true God. Nevertheless, the first gods were perishable gods. Their worship came to its inevitable end. They lost their efficacy by the benediction of the Lord of Heaven, after the redemption of the world was accomplished, after the resurrection of the true God, the true Dios, when he blessed heaven and earth. Then was your worship abolished, Maya men. Turn away your hearts from your old religion.

This is the history of the world in those times, because it has been written down, because the time has not yet ended for making these books, these many explanations, so that Maya men may be asked if they know how they were born here in this country, when the land was founded.

It was Katun 11 Ahau when the *Ah Mucenca* came forth to blindfold the faces of the Oxlahun-ti-ku; but they did not know his name, except for his older sister and his sons. They said his face had not yet been shown to them also. This was after the creation of the world had been completed, but they did not know it was about to occur. Then Oxlahun-ti-ku was seized by Bolon-ti-ku. Then it was that fire descended, then the rope descended, then rocks and trees descended. Then came the beating of things with wood and stone. Then Oxlahun-ti-ku was seized, his head was wounded, his face was buffeted, he was spit upon, and he was thrown on his back as well. After that he was despoiled of his insignia and his smut. Then shoots of the yaxum tree were taken. Also Lima beans were taken with crumbled tubercles, hearts of small squash-seeds, large squash-seeds and beans, all crushed. He wrapped up the seeds composing this first Bolon ¢acab, and went to the thirteenth heaven. Then a mass of maize-dough with the tips of corn-cobs remained here on earth. Then its heart departed because of Oxlahun-ti-ku, but they did not know the heart of the tubercle was gone. After that the fatherless ones, the miserable ones, and those without husbands were all pierced through; they were alive though they had no hearts. Then they were buried in the sands, in the sea.

There would be a sudden rush of water when the theft of the insignia of Oxlahun-ti-ku occurred. Then the sky would fall, it would fall down upon the earth, when the four gods, the four Bacabs, were set up, who brought about the destruction of the world. Then, after the destruction of the world was completed, they placed a tree to set up in its order the yellow cock oriole. Then the white tree of abundance was set up. A pillar of the sky was set up, a sign of the destruction of the world; that was the white tree of abundance in the north. Then the black tree of abundance was set up in the west for the black-breasted *pi¢oy* to sit upon. Then the yellow tree of abundance was set up in the south , as a symbol of the destruction of the world, for the yellow-breasted *pi¢oy* to sit upon, for the yellow cock oriole to sit upon, the yellow timid *mut*. Then the green tree of abundance was set up in the center of the world as a record of the destruction of the world.

The plate of another katun was set up and fixed in its place by the messengers of their lord. The red Piltec was set at the east of the world to conduct people to his lord. The white Piltec was set at the north of the world to conduct people to his lord. Lahun Chaan was set at the west to bring things to his lord. The yellow Piltec was set at the south to bring things to his lord. But it was over the whole world that Ah Uuc Cheknal was set up. He came from the seventh stratum of the earth, when he came to fecundate Itzam-kab-ain, when he came with the vitality of the angle between earth and heaven. They moved among the four lights, among the four layers of the stars. The world was not lighted; there was neither day nor night nor moon. Then they perceived that the world was being created. Then creation dawned upon the world. ✠ During the creation thirteen infinite series added to seven was the count of the creation of the world. Then a new world dawned for them.

The two-day throne was declared, the three-day throne. Then began the weeping of Oxlahun-ti-ku. They wept in this reign. The reign became red; the mat became red; the first tree of the world was rooted fast. The entire world was proclaimed by Uuc-yol-zip; but it was not at the time of this reign that Bolon-ti-ku-wept. Then came the counting of the mat in its order. Red was the mat on which Bolon-ti-ku sat. His buttock is sharply rounded, as he sits on his mat. Then descended greed from the heart of the sky, greed for power, greed for rule.

Then the red foundation was established; the white foundation of the ruler was established; the black foundation was established; the yellow foundation was established. Then the Red Ruler was set up, he who was raised upon the mat, raised upon the throne. The White Ruler was set up, he who was raised upon the mat, raised upon the throne. The Black Ruler was set up, he who was raised upon the mat, raised upon the throne. The Yellow Ruler was set up, he who was raised upon the mat, raised upon the throne.

As a god, it is said; whether or not gods, their bread is lacking, their water is lacking.

There was only a portion of what was needed for them to eat together . . . but there was nowhere from which the quantity needed for existence could come. Compulsion and force were the tidings, when he was seated in authority ; compulsion was the tidings, compulsion by misery; it came during his reign, when he arrived to sit upon the mat ... Suddenly on high fire flamed up. The face of the sun was snatched away, taken from earth. This was his garment in his reign. This was the reason for mourning his power, at that time there was too much vigor. At that time there was the riddle for the rulers. The planted timber was set up. Perishable things are assembled at that time. The timber of the grave-digger is set up at the crossroads, at the four resting places. Sad is the general havoc, at that time the butterflies swarmed. Then there came great misery, when it came about that the sun in

Katun 3 Ahau was moved from its place for three months. After three years it will come back into place in Katun 3 Ahau. Then another katun will beset in its place . The *ramon* fruit is their bread, the *ramon* fruit is their drink; the *jícama cimarrona* is their bread, the *jícama cimarrona* is their drink; what they eat and what they drink. The *ix-batun*, the *chimchim-chay*, are what they eat. These things were present here when misery settled, father, in Tun 9. At that time there were the foreigners. The charge of misery was sought for all the years of Katun 13 Ahau.

Then it was that the lord of Katun 11 Ahau spread his feet apart. Then it was that the word of Bolon ¢acab descended to the tip of his tongue. Then the charge of the katun was sought; nine was its charge when it descended from heaven. Kan was the day when its burden was bound to it. Then the water descended, it came from the heart of the sky for the baptism of the House of Nine Bushes. With it descended Bolon Mayel; sweet was his mouth and the tip of his tongue. Sweet were his brains. Then descended the four mighty supernatural jars, this was the honey of the flowers.

Then there grew up for it the red unfolded calyx, the white unfolded calyx, the black unfolded calyx and the yellow unfolded calyx, those which were half a palm broad and those which were a whole palm in breadth . Then there sprang up the five-leafed flower, the five drooping petals , the cacao with grains like a row of teeth, the *ix-chabil-tok*, the little flower, Ix Macuil Xuchit, the flower with the brightly colored tip, the *laurel* flower, and the limping flower. After these flowers sprang up, there were the vendors of fragrant odors, there was the mother of the flowers. Then there sprang up the bouquet of the priest, the bouquet of the ruler, the bouquet of the captain; this was what the flower-king bore when he descended and nothing else, so they say. It was not bread that he bore. Then it was that the flower sprang up, wide open, to introduce the sin of Bolon-ti-ku. After three years was the time when he said he did not come to create Bolon ¢acab as the god in hell. Then descended Ppizlimtec to take the flower; he took the figure of a humming-bird with green plumage on its breast, when he descended. Then he sucked the honey from the flower with nine petals. Then the five-petaled flower took him for her husband, Thereupon the heart of the flower came forth to set itself in motion. Four-fold was the plate of the flower, and Ah Kin Xocbiltun was set in the center. At this time Oxlahun-ti-ku came forth, but he did not know of the descent of the sin of the mat, when he came into his power. The flower was his mat, the flower was his chair. He sat in envy, he walked in envy. Envy was his plate, envy was his cup. There was envy in his heart, in his understanding, in his thought and in his speech. Ribald and insolent was his speech during his reign. At that time his food cries out, his drink cries out, from the corner of his mouth when he eats, from the back of his claw when he bites his food. He holds in his hand a piece of wood, he holds in his hand a stone. Mighty are his teeth; his face is that of Lahun Chan, as he sits. Sin is in his face, in his speech, in his talk, in his understanding and in his walk. His eyes are blindfolded. He seizes, he demands as his right, the mat on which he sits during his reign. Forgotten is his father, forgotten is his mother, nor does his mother know her offspring. The heart is on fire alone in the fatherless one who despises his father, in the motherless one. He shall walk abroad giving the appearance of one drunk, without understanding, in company with his father, in company with his mother. There is no virtue in him, there is no goodness in his heart, only a little on the tip of his tongue. He does not know in what manner his end is to come; nor does he know what will be the end of his reign, when the period of his power shall terminate.

This is Bolon-ti-ku. Like that of Bolon Chan is the face of the ruler of men, the two day occupant of the mat and throne. He came in Katun 3 Ahau. After that there will be another lord of the land who will establish the law of another katun, after the law of the lord of Katun 3 Ahau shall have run its course. At that time there shall be few children; then there shall be mourning among the Itza who speak our language brokenly. Industry and vigor finally take the place, in the first tun of the new katun , of the sin of the Itzá who speak our language brokenly. It is Bolon-ti-ku who shall come to his end with the law of the lord of Katun 3 Ahau. Then the riddle of the rulers of the land shall end the law of the katun. Then those of the lineage of the noble chiefs shall come into their own, with the other men of discretion and with those of the lineage of the chiefs. Their faces had been trampled on the ground, and they had been overthrown by the unrestrained upstarts of the day and of the katun, the son of evil and the offspring of the harlot, who were born when their day dawned in Katun 3 Ahau. Thus shall end the power of those who are two-faced toward our Lord God.

XI

(THE RITUAL OF THE ANGELS)

Dominus vobiscum ended the words of their song when there was neither heaven nor earth. When the world was submerged, when there was neither heaven nor earth, the three-cornered precious stone of grace was born, after the divinity of the ruler was created, when there was no heaven. Then there were born seven tuns, seven katuns, hanging in the heart of the wind, the seven chosen ones. Then, they say, their seven graces stirred also. Seven also were their holy images. While they were still untarnished, occurred the birth of the first precious stone of grace, the first infinite grace, when there was infinite night, when there was no God. Not yet had he received his Godhead. Then he remained alone within the grace, within the night, when there was neither heaven nor earth. Then he departed at the end of the katun, as he could not be born in the first katun. There were his long locks of hair, *adeu ti paramir*, his divinity came to him when he departed.

Thereupon he became man in the second infinite precious stone of grace. Then there arrived in the second katun Alpilcon, as the angel was named when he was born. The second grace was permitted to depart in the second infinite night, when no one was present. Then he received his divinity, alone and through his own effort, when he came to depart. "*O firmar*" he said, when he received his divinity by himself and through his own effort.

Thereupon he departed and went to the third infinite precious stone of grace. Alba Congel was the name of its angel. This was the third grace.

Let me proceed to the fourth infinite precious stone of grace, to the fourth night. Atea Ohe was the name of its angel. The fourth grace was born and began to speak, alone and through his own effort. "Oh god, the ruler! I am after all nothing in myself." These were his words in his concealment, in his divinity within the grace. "Let me still proceed," he said.

Then he went to the fifth infinite precious stone of grace, to the fifth infinite night. The fifth grace was born in the fifth katun. Thereupon he was set up to declare his divinity. Then his angel was born; Decipto was the name of his angel when he was set up. "Since it is so, let me go. Who might I be? I am a god, a ruler, after all," and he declared his divinity all alone. "*A ninite dei sin*," he said when he received his divinity all by himself.

Then he went to the sixth infinite precious stone of grace, to the sixth measured night, to the sixth katun: "Ye gods, ye rulers! Make answer to my words. After all, I am nothing in myself alone."

The seventh grace was born. Conlamil was the name of his angel. "I deliver the things of god to you who are gods. Answer my words. After all, there is no one; no one replies to my words." Thus he spoke as he caused the seventh grace to be born. And there was joy in his heart at the birth of the seventh katun, the seven lights, the seventh measured night and the seven infinite things .

39

Abiento bocayento de la zipil na de fente note. Sustina gracia, trece mili, uno cargo bende. The first, the second, the thirteenth unfolding; thirteen banners of the katuns; three, seven, eight thousand. Then God the Father awoke to consciousness alone in person; in the three-cornered precious stone of grace he awoke to consciousness, God the Father, as his name was known to be. *Unidad* and God the Father, these were his names, cleft from the katun for you. There were three generations suddenly augmented in stature when he came. Seven were the generations of his angels. Four times did he first speak. There was one seal in the darkness, one seal on high. "I am the beginning and I shall be the end." Here are his words in their mighty entirety. "*Datate* here to that which has been received. I am *Unidate, I am also Unitata,* I am the Dove, I am *Unitata Anuni. Unidad* cometh."

Nilu was the name of the night. This was the first speech of God; this was the first speech of the Father. Of cleansed stone was his precious stone alone in the night. *Etomas,* Çipancas was the name of the wind. Hun Katun was his father. *Otahocanil Aucangel* was the name of the wind. H i eron was the name of the Wind. Xicluto-tu-tanil was the name of the wind. Virtutus was the name of the wind. Joramis was the name of the wind in the second katun. This was what he said when he changed the stone: "*Jaxyonlacalpa.*" He covered the name of the holy heaven which our holy Lord, the Father raised up. Bolay was the name of the serpent of the second heaven. He was in the dust at the feet of *Sustinal Gracia,* as he was called. Then Lonmias was formed. The sharp stone was his stone within the night. Zihontun was his stone, when these stones were fixed in their places. Three times they were set at the foot of *Sustinal Gracia.* These stones were born, they were beneath the one stone, the mighty pointed stone, the stone column, the mighty pointed clashing stone. They were manifested all over the world by God the Father, the first ruler. In the first katun was born the only son of God; in the second katun, the Father. In the third katun was *Expleo-ucaan,* as he was called, who chastised him named *Chac Opilla* when he set up the heavens. *Enpileo-u-caan* was his name. *Expleo* was his name within the first noose of God. Hebones was the only son of God. Like a mirror he was borne astride on the shoulder of his father, on the stone of his father.

Then, it is said, the boldness of the heaven on high was created. This was one grace, one stone; then fire was created, Tixitate was his name, the light of the heavens. Sustinal, they say, was the light from that which lighted the heaven. Acpa, it was, who made the katun after the light originated in the heavens. Alpa-u-manga was his name after it ended.

These are the angels of the winds which were set up while he created the star, when the world was not yet lighted, when there was neither heaven nor earth: the Red Pauahtun, the White Pauahtun, the Black Pauahtun, the Yellow Pauahtun.

Here was the first heaven where God the Father was set up, grasping in his hand his stone, grasping his *cangel,* grasping his wheel on which are hung the four angels of the winds. Cerpinus was the name of him who, under Orele, measured the land. They were three persons, God the Father, God the Son and God the Holy Spirit. He set up the planets, Saturn, Jupiter, Mars, Venus, which he said were held in the grasp of the god in heaven when he created them. This was the name of the heaven, cristalino. Here were the Angels. Corpinus was the name of him who held aloft on the palm of his hand the

Blessed Father when there was neither heaven nor earth. Inpicco was his name when all the angels were asperged. Baloyo was his name when the water was sprinkled. Seros was his name, *Et sepeuas. Laus Deo.*

Below were Chac Bolay Balam and the cacao called *balamté.* Esperas was the name of the sixth heaven; Isperas was the name of the seventh heaven. Then the world was created by God the ruler in the seventh katun, created in the darkness named Espiritu. St. Edendeus and St. Eluceo were the saints who witnessed the birth of him who was hidden within the stone, hidden within the night. *Se repite elitun entri de noche.* These were the words said by him who was hidden within the stone, hidden within the night: *Tronas Aleseyo de mundo de gracia. En apedia tejo çipi dia te en pieted gracia. Santo Esuleptun jam estum est gracia. Suplilis el timeo me firme abin finitis gracia, y metis absolutum ti metis de gracia. Abegintis gracia, Edendeo gracia, de fentis de gracia, fenoplis tun gracia. Locom dar yme gracia, tretris u mis gracia. Noçi luçi de gracia, in pricio de gracia, trese mili uno de cargo, leonte."*

One, two, thirteen, one division, thirteen *bakam* of katuns. Three, seven, eight thousand was the creation of the world, when he who was hidden within the stone, hidden within the night, was born, when there was neither heaven nor earth. Then God the Father spoke alone, by his own efforts, in the darkness that clung like a thrice withered fruit to the tree . This was the first word of God, when there was neither heaven nor earth, when he came out of the stone and fell into the second stone. Then it was that he declared his divinity. Then resounded eight thousand katuns at the word of the first stone of grace, the first ornamented stone of grace. It was the macaw that warmed it well behind the *acantun.*

Who was born when our father descended?

Thou knowest. There was born the first macaw who cast the stones behind the *acantun.*

How was the grain of maize born? How, indeed, father?

Thou knowest. The tender green shoot was born in heaven.

"Ciripacte, horca mundo. Ni mompan est noche. Amanena, omonena, apa opa," was said when the wind emerged from the great stone of grace. *"Cipiones ted coruna, pater profecido,"* were his words when he arrived at the seventh stratum of the solid rock of grace. *"Bal te piones, orteçipio, reçi quenta noche. Hun ebrietate, hun cute profeciado,"* were the words of the Angel, Jerupiter. Then the sky was put in its place, *Corporales ti ojales,* by the first pope, the face of the katun, the burden of the Katun 13 Ahau. The face of the sun shall be turned from its course, it shall be turned face down during the reign of the perishable men, the perishable rulers. Five days the sun is eclipsed, and then shall be seen the torch of Katun 13 Ahau, a sign given by God that death shall come to the rulers of this land. Thus it shall come about that the first rulers are driven from their towns. Then Christianity shall have come here to the land.

Thus it is that God, our Father, gives a sign when they shall come, because there is no agreement. The descendants of the former rulers are dishonored and brought to misery; we are christianized, while they treat us like animals. There is sorrow in the heart of God because of these "suckers."

In the year Fifteen hundred and thirty-nine, 1539, to the east was the door of the House of Don Juan Montejo, to introduce Christianity here to the land of Yucalpeten, Yucatan.

Chilam Balam, the prophet.

Thus today is not an unlucky day . . .

This was his name, God the Father, when he came to exist in person, after the creation of the world and the earth. This was then his name.

Joshua was his second name. In his third person, his name for the third time was Mesister in Latin, Dei in the vernacular.

The Red Pauahtun was Utcorusis.

The White Pauahtun was Corocalbo.

The Black Pauahtun was Corusi-provento.

The Yellow Pauahtun was Moses.

No vis.

No va.

Messiah was the name of God before the heavens and the earth were created. Messiah the Christ, was his name. Then he created the Angels. But it was manifested to God that half of the Angels were destined to sin.

The second name of God was Emanuel. To this was added his third name; this then was Jeremiah, his name when there was neither heaven nor earth.

The misspelled Latin and Spanish names may have been taken from some Spanish treatise on astrology or magic. The decoration here is evidently borrowed from some Spanish religious book.

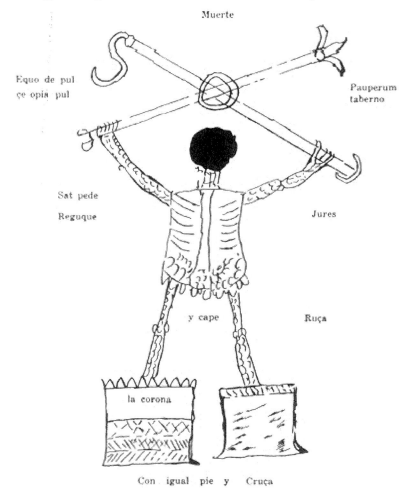

Muerte

Equo de pul
çe opia pul

Pauperum
taberno

Sat pede
Reguque

Jures

y cape

Ruça

la corona

Con igual pie y Cruça

But when the law of the katun shall have run its course, then God will bring about a great deluge again which will be the end of the world. When this is over, then our Lord Jesus Christ shall descend over the valley of Jehoshaphat beside the town of Jerusalem where he redeemed us with his holy

43

blood. He shall descend on a great cloud to bear true testimony that he was once obliged to suffer, stretched out on a cross of wood. Then shall descend in his great power and glory the true God who created heaven and earth and everything on earth. He shall descend to level off the world for the good and the bad, the conquerors and the captives.

XII

(A SONG OF THE ITZÁ)

Damascus was the name of the plain where our first father, Adam, was created by God. This was his name, his first name was Adam, after his soul entered into him , after Paradise was set up. After Adam had then been created, then was created our first mother, Eve, the first woman, the mother of the whole world. Drops of moisture formed on the stones and bushes for the first time, they say, created when there was no sky.

But God the Father was created alone and by his own effort in the darkness. But the stones were created separately. This was the land of Acantun. This was created after Adam was formed also. They were put in the place where the Acans are. Thus it was that he named them when he created them all. These were the first people.

God the Father, God the Son and God the Holy Spirit, these are the joint names of God. They were created in the stone, the red slender stone and the worn stone of grace. His name is the Word, Josustin Graçia.

However, at the same time there was born in the stone, the black stone of terror, the one named Verbum-tuorum, Ix-coal-tun, Ix-coal-cab, taken by the mistress of the world. Then there was set in its place the thrice seasoned heaven, the seasoned heaven. White and clean, it lay guarded in the heart of *Sustinal Gracia*. Thirteen orders of katuns lay prostrate in the stone. Then the ruler, Hunac Ceel, stirred into motion.

The song: Ho! What is so precious as we are? It is the precious jewel worn on the breast. Ho! What is the distinction of righteous men? It is my mantle, my loin-cloth. So spoke the god. Then do you mourn for anyone?

No one. A tender boy was I at Chichen, when the evil man, the master of the army, came to seize the land. Woe!

At Chichen Itzá heresy was favored! *Yulu uayano!* Ho! 1 Imix was the day when the ruler was seized at Chikin-chen. Ho! Where thou art, there is the god. Ho! 1 Imix was the day he said this. At Chichen Itzá heresy was favored! Yulu uayano! Buried, buried! This was their cry. Buried, buried! This they also knew . . . This also was their cry on that first day of Yaxkin, that mighty day, 2 Akbal, they came. Woe! Woe! Woe! *Yulu uayano!* Is there perhaps anyone who by chance has awakened? Force was brought to bear for the second time. Woe! For the third time was established the religious festival of our enemies, our enemies. *Uuiyao!* Soon it will come to Chichen Itzá, where heresy was favored. *Yulu uayano!* In the third heaven is the sun. Behold! Who am I said to be among men? I am a leafy covering. Eya! Who am I among the people of Putun? You do not understand me. *Eya!* I was created in the night. What were we born? *Eya!* We were like tame animals to Mizcit Ahau. But an end comes to his roguery. Behold, so I remember my song. Heresy was favored. *Yulu uayano*! *Eya*! I die, he said, because of the town festival. *Eya*! I shall come, he said, because of the destruction of the town. This is the end of what is in his mind, of what he thought in his heart. Me, he did not destroy. I tell what I have remembered in my song. Heresy was favored. *Yulu uayano*!

This is all of the song, the completion of the message of the Lord God.

XIII

(THE CREATION OF THE UINAL)

Thus it was recorded by the first sage, Melchise dek , the first prophet, Napuc Tun, the priest, the first priest. This is a song of how the *uinal* came to be created before the creation of the world. Then he began to march by his own effort alone. Then said his maternal grandmother, then said his maternal aunt, then said his paternal grandmother, then said his sister-in-law: "What shall we say when we see man on the road?" These were their words as they marched along, when there was no man as yet . Then they arrived there in the east and began to speak. "Who has passed here? Here are footprints. Measure it off with your foot." So spoke the mistress of the world. Then he measured the footstep of our Lord, God the Father. This was the reason it was called counting off the whole earth, *lahca* (12) Oc. This was the count, after it had been created by the day 13 Oc, after his feet were joined evenly, after they had departed there in the east. Then he spoke its name when the day had no name, after he had marched along with his maternal grandmother, his maternal aunt, his paternal grandmother and his sister-in-law. The uinal was created, the day, as it was called, was created, heaven and earth were created, the stairway of water, the earth, rocks and trees; the things of the sea and the things of the land were created.

On 1 Chuen he raised himself to his divinity, after he had made heaven and earth.

On 2 Eb he made the first stairway. It descended from the midst of the heavens, in the midst of the water, when there were neither earth, rocks nor trees.

On 3 Ben he made all things, as many as there are, the things of the heavens, the things of the sea and the things of the earth.

On 4 Ix sky and earth were tilted.

On 5 Men he made everything.

On 6 Cib the first candle was made; it became light when there was neither sun nor moon.

On 7 Caban honey was first created, when we had none.

On 8 E¢nab his hand and foot were firmly set, then he picked up small things on the ground.

On 9 Cauac hell was first considered.

On 10 Ahau wicked men went to hell because of God the Father, that they might not be noticed.

On 11 Imix rocks and trees were formed; this he did within the day.

On 12 Ik the breath of life was created. The reason it was called Ik was because there was no death in it.

On 13 Akbal he took water and watered the ground. Then he shaped it and it became man.

On 1 Kan he first created anger because of the evil he had created.

On 2 Chicchan occurred the discovery of whatever evil he saw within the town.

On 3 Cimi he invented death; it happened that our Lord God invented the first death.

On 5 Lamat he established the seven great waters of the sea.

On 6 Muluc all valleys were submerged, when the world was not yet created. Then occurred the invention of the word of our Lord God, when there was no word in heaven, when there were neither rocks nor trees.

Then they went to consider what they were , and the voice spoke as follows:

"Thirteen entities, seven entities, one." So it spoke when the word came forth, at the time when there was no word. Then the reason was sought by the first ruling day (the first day Ahau) why the meaning of the word to them was not revealed so that they could declare themselves. Then they went to the center of heaven and joined hands. Then the following were set up in the middle of the land: the Burners, four of them:

4 Chicchan,	the Burner.
4 Oc,	the Burner.
4 Men,	the Burner.
4 Ahau,	the Burner.

These are the four Rulers.

8 Muluc		5 Cauac
9 Oc		6 Ahau
10 Chuen	2	7 Imix

11 Eb		8 Ik
12 Ben	4	9 Akbal
13 Ix	5	10 Kan
1 Men	6	11 Chicchen
2 Cib		12 Cimi
3 Caban	7	13 Manik
4 E¢nab		1 Lamat ,

The day-name Oc is a homonym for the word meaning foot. Ix has a slight resemblance to the root of *nixpahal* meaning to tilt. Men means to make or to do something. The syllable *e¢* of E¢nab means to set something firmly on the ground. Nevertheless the Maya were not unaware of the relation between this day and the flint knife pictured by its glyph, for in another manuscript we find it associated with a flint, as well as with the blood-letter and the warrior, both of whom employed this implement (Kaua, p. 21).

The association of the day Ahau with hell (*metnal*) may be because of its resemblance to that of Cumhau (or Hun Ahau,) one of the names of the god of the underworld and whom the author of the Motul Dictionary identifies as "Lucifer, the prince of the devils." Akbal is associated with the verb *akzah*, which means to water the ground. Chicchan resembles *chictahal* which means to find. The day-name Cimi and the Maya word meaning death are homonyms. Muluc resembles the verb *mucchahal* meaning to be buried or submerged.}

The uinal was created, the earth was created; sky, earth, trees and rocks were set in order; all things were created by our Lord God, the Father.

Thus he was there in his divinity, in the clouds, alone and by his own effort, when he created the entire world, when he moved in the heavens in his divinity. Thus he ruled in his great power. Every day is set in order according to the count, beginning in the east, as it is arranged.

XIV

(A HISTORY OF THE SPANISH CONQUEST)

This is the name of the year when the foreigners arrived, the year One thousand five hundred and nineteen. This was the year when the foreigners arrived here at our town, the town of us, the Itzá, here in the land of Yucalpeten, Yucatan, in the speech of the Maya Itzá.

So said the first Adelantado; Don Juan de Montejo, because he was thus informed by Don Lorenso Chable when he listened to this conqueror at Tixkokob. He received the foreigners with all his heart. This was the reason they named him Don Lorenso Chable, because he gave well-roasted meat to the foreigners and all the captains. He had a son also named Don Martin Chable.

This is the year which was current when the foreigners prepared to seize *Yucalpeten* here. It was known by the priest, the prophet, Ah Xupan, as he was called. Christianity was introduced to us in the year 1519. The church at Merida was founded in the year 1540. In the year 1599 the church at

Merida was completed. In the year 1648 yellow fever occurred and the sickness began to afflict us.

There was death by famine for five years, 1650, 1651, 1652, 1653 and 1654. Then the famine ended. There was a hurricane which killed Father Agustin Gomes in the year 1661. There was a drought in the year 1669. The disease called *uzankak* occurred in 1692.

XV

(THE PROPHECY OF CHILAM BALAM AND THE STORY OF ANTONIO MARTINEZ)

Let it be known that the day then arrived when the tenth katun was established, when the katun of the Plumeria flower was established. For three moons had been established Yuma-une-tziuit, the quetzal, the green bird. Then there shall be present the forceful one, there would be Nine Mountains, Yuma-une-tziuit, the quetzal, the green bird. No one understands the penance among the rulers in the twelfth tun when he declared his name. Like a jaguar is his head, long is his tooth, withered is his body, like a dog is his body. His heart is pierced with sorrow. Sweet is his food, sweet is his drink. Perchance he does not speak, perchance he will not hear. They say his speech is false and mad. Nowhere do the younger sisters, native to the land, surrender themselves. They shall be taken away from the land here. So it shall always be with the maidens, the daughters whom they shall bear tomorrow and day after tomorrow. Give yourselves up, my younger brothers, my older brothers, submit to the unhappy destiny of the katun which is to come. If you do not submit, you shall be moved from where your feet are rooted. If you do not submit, you shall gnaw the trunks of trees and herbs. If you do not submit, it shall be as when the deer die, so that they go forth from your settlement. Then even when the ruler himself goes forth, he shall return within your settlement bearing nothing. Also there shall come such a pestilence that the vultures enter the houses, a time of great death among the wild animals. There shall be three kinds of bread, the bread-nut shall be their bread in the katun of the Plumeria flower. Then comes the time when thirteen layers of mats are laid down for the very mad one, for the adulterer. Then comes the papal bull of six divisions. Three times the bull shall be announced. Then the judge of the bull shall come, when he who bears the gold staff shall judge, when white wax candles shall be exchanged. It is to be white wax, when justice shall descend from Heaven, for Christian men to come up before the eye of justice. Then it shall shake heaven and earth. In sorrow shall end the katun of the Plumeria flower. No one shall fulfil his promises. The prop-roots of the trees shall be bent over. There shall be an earthquake all over the land. The fulfilment of the prophecy of the katun of the Plumeria flower shall be for sale. There is no reason or necessity for you to submit to the Archbishop. When he comes, you shall go and hide yourselves in the forest. If you surrender yourselves, you shall follow Christ, when he shall come. Then his visitation shall end. Then shall come to pass the shaking of the Plumeria flower. Then you shall understand. Then it shall thunder from a dry sky. Then shall be spoken that which is written on the wall. Then you shall set up God, that is, you shall admit his divinity to your hearts. I hardly know what wise man among you will understand. He who understands will go into the forest to serve Christianity. Who will understand it?

After only fourteen years of chieftainship, permanently the Son shall arrive, Don Antonio Martínez and Saul. These were his names when he departed from heaven. At that time he went to Tzimentan, and when he was at Tzimentan a certain queen said she would marry him. For seven years he was married, when the golden doors of the house of four apartments were opened. Here he was shown how, and he equipped a fleet of thirteen ships. Then he began a war with the land of Havana. The King had a friend at Havana, and the King was advised by his friend. The public prosecutor was there with him. Then he went and heard that the man was to be seized. Whereupon he departed and went to Tzimentan. It was three months after he was seized that the man who took him departed. Then he arrived at Tzimentan. When the man was seized, he cut short the words of him who took him when he arrived at Tzimentan, and he said: "Go, man." These were his words to him. "It is three months since I arrived," he said. "It is three months, now, since you departed. It was three months ago that you arrived, since you arrived, since you are shut up in the prison; in the meantime I come. I will take you out of prison. You two captains shall follow me." he said.

"Let nine chairs be raised up for us to sit on. The sea shall burn. I shall be raised up." There was fire in his eye. Sand and spray shall be raised aloft. The face of the sun shall be darkened by the great tempest. Whereupon the captain accoutered himself. Everything shall be blown to the ground by the wind. In the meantime I sit on my chair; in the meantime the fleet of thirteen ships comes. Then the King accouters himself also. "Prepare yourself, my lord! There come the French." These were his words to me. "We shall be killed by these men. For what reason does your strength fail because of your compatriots? Let me go and direct the ship from the middle." My own spirits are raised also. The sea upon which I go burns. The face of the heavens is tilted. But when I came down into his presence, the ship was lost. "What man are you?" he said to me. "I am without compunction. It is I whom you have aided, I am he whom you have caused to live again." Then he said: "I shall put my name to the test, it is Martinez. God the Father, God the Son, God the Holy Spirit is my name." These were his words. Then I brought out the book of seven generations to read. In three months it was finished.

Now the town officials went elsewhere. Whereupon he said he would give his town, half of the men in it, to me. "Where is your town? It is all my town," he said . "You shall pay for my town, I was the first to arrive." Then, I tell you, justice shall descend to the end that Christianity and salvation may arise. Thus shall end the men of the Plumeria flower. Then the rulers of the towns shall be asked for their proofs and titles of ownership, if they know of them. Then they shall come forth from the forests and from among the rocks and live like men; then towns shall be established again . There shall be no fox to bite them. This shall be in Katun 9 Ahau. Five years shall run until the end of my prophecy, and then shall come the time for the tribute to come down. Then there shall be an end to the paying for the wars which our fathers raised against the Spaniards . You shall not call the katun which is to come a hostile one, when Jesus Christ, the guardian of our souls, shall come. Just as we are saved here on earth, so shall he bear our souls to his holy heaven also. You are sons of the true God. Amen.

XVI

(A CHAPTER OF QUESTIONS AND ANSWERS)

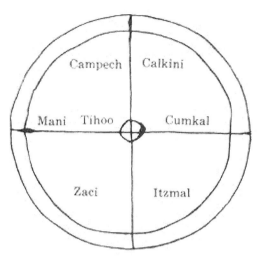

13 E¢nab was the day when the land was established. 13 Cheneb was when they measured off by paces the cathedral, the dark house of instruction, the cathedral in heaven. Thus it was also measured off by paces here on earth . Thirteen katuns was the total count, that is, thir teen feet in heaven. Four feet, and from there nine feet, the total count of its extent in heaven. Then it is again measured off by feet from the face of the earth. Four feet separate it from the face of the earth.

Mani is the base of the land. Campeche is the tip of the wing of the land. Calkini is the base of the wing of the land. Itzmal is the middle of the wing of the land. Zaci is the tip of the wing of the land. Conkal is the head of the land.

In the middle of the town of Tihoo is the cathedral, the fiery house, the mountainous house, the dark house, for the benefit of God the Father, God the Son and God the Holy Spirit.

Who enters into the house of God? Father, it is the one named Ix-Kalem.

What day did the Virgin conceive? Father, 4 Oc was the day when she conceived.

What day did he come forth from her womb ? On 3 Oc he came forth.

What day did he die? On 1 Cimi he died. Then he entered the tomb on 1 Cimi.

What entered his tomb? Father, a coffer of stone entered his tomb.

What entered in into his thigh? Father, it was the red arrow-stone. It entered into the precious stone of the world, there in heaven.

And his arm? Father, the arrow-stone; and that it might be commemorated, it entered into the red living rock in the east. Then it came to the north and entered into the white living rock. After that it entered the black living rock in the west. Thus also it entered the yellow living rock in the south.

Son, how many deep hollows are there ? These are the holes for playing the flute.

Son, where is the cenote? All are drenched with its water. There is no gravel on its bottom; a bow is inserted over its entrance. It is the church.

Son, where are the first marriages? The strength of the King and the strength of the other head-chiefs fail because of them, and my strength because of them also. It is bread.

Son, have you seen the green water-holes in the rock? There are two of them; a cross is raised between them. They are a man's eyes.

Son, where are the first baptised ones? One has no mother, but has a bead collar and little bells. It is *peeu*.

Son, where is the food which bursts forth, and the fold of the brain and the lower end of that which is inflated, and the dried fruit? It is the gizzard of a turkey.

Son bring me that which hooks the sky and the hooked tooth. They are a deer and a gopher.

Son, where is the old woman with buttocks seven palms wide, the woman with a dark complexion? It is the squash called *¢ol*.

Son, show me the light complexioned woman with her skirt bound up who sells white flints. It is the squash called *ca*.

Son, bring me two yellow animals, one to be well boiled, and one shall have its throat cut. I shall drink its blood also. It is a yellow deer and a green calabash full of chocolate.

My sons, bring me here a score of those who bear flat stones and two married ones. They are a quail and a dove.

Son, bring me a cord of three strands, I wish to see it. It is an iguana.

Son, bring . . . . a mutual confession of sin that I may see it here. It is the maguey.

Son, bring me here that which stops the hole in the sky and the dew, the nine layers of the whole earth. It is a very large maize tortilla.

Son, have you seen the old man who is like an overturned *comal*? He has a large double chin which reaches the ground. It is a turkey cock.

Son, bring me the old farmers, their beards come to their navels, also their wives. It is a muddy arrowroot.

Bring to me here with them the women who guard the fields, white complexioned women. I will remove their skirts and eat them. It is a jícama.

Son, bring me the great gallants that I may view them. Perhaps they will not dance badly when I see them. It is a turkey-cock.

Son, where is the first collector? The answer is to undress, to take off one's shirt, cape, hat and shoes.

Son, where was it that you passed? Did you pass, perchance, to the high rocky knoll which slopes down to the door of heaven, where there is a gate in the wall? Did you see men in front of you, coming side by side? Bolon Chaan and the first *Ah-kulel* are there. It is the pupils of the eyes and any pair of eyes.

Son, have you seen the rain of God? It passed beneath the mountains of God; it entered beneath the mountains of God, where there is a cross on the savannah. There will be a ring in the sky where the water of God has passed.

Son, where has the water of God passed when it comes forth from the living rock? Father, from a man's head and all a man's teeth, it passes through the opening in his throat and comes forth beneath.

Son, whom did you see on the road just now? . . . .

Son, what did you do with your companions who were coming close behind you? Here are my companions. I have not left them. I await the judgment of God when I shall come to die. This is a man's shadow.

Son, whom did you see on the road? Did you see perchance some old men accompanied by their boys? Father, here are the old men I saw on the road. They are with me; they do not leave me. This is his great toe with the little toes .

Son, where did you see the old women carrying their step-children and their other boys. Father, here they are. They are still with me so that I can eat. I can not leave them yet. It is my thumb and the other fingers.

Son, where did you pass by a water-gutter? Father, here is the water-gutter; it is right with me. This is my dorsal furrow.

Son, where did you see an old man astride a horse across a water-gutter? Father, here is the old man. He is still with me. My shoulders are the horse on which you say the old man sits astride.

Son, this is the old man with you of which you spoke: it is manifest truth and justice.

Son, go get the heart of the stone and the liver of the earth. . . . I have seen one of them lying on its back, and one lying on its face as though it were going into hell. They are a Mexican Agouti and a Spotted Agouti, also the first local chief and the first Ah-kulel. As for the heart of the stone, it is the tips of the teeth; and that which covers the opening in the neck of hell is a camote and a jícama.

Son, go and bring me here the girl with the watery teeth. Her hair is twisted into a tuft; she is a very beautiful maiden. Fragrant shall be her odor when I remove her skirt and her other garment. It will give me pleasure to see her. Fragrant is her odor and her hair is twisted into a tuft. It is an ear of green corn cooked in a pit.

Son, then you shall go and get an old man and the herb that is by the sea. The old man is the *ac*, and the herb is a crab.

Son, then you shall go and get the stones from the bottom of a forest pond. It is the *tzac*.

Son, then you shall bring here the stones of the savannah. It is a quail.

Also bring the first sorcerers, there are four of them. They are the gopher, the Spotted Agouti, the Mexican Agouti and the peccary.

Son, then go and get the thigh of the earth. It is the cassava.

Son, go and bring here the green gallant and the green singer. It is a wild turkey hen and cock.

Son, you shall bring your daughter that I may see her in the sun tomorrow. First the smaller one shall be brought and behind her shall come the larger one. Her hair shall be bound with a feathered band; she shall wear a head-scarf. I will take off her head-scarf. Also the Ah-kulel is behind her.

Son, then go and get a cluster of Plumeria flowers widely separated. They should be there where the sun is tomorrow. What is meant is roasted corn and honey.

Here I have rolled that which you have which is flat and round. There are many rolls of it in the cave where you live. Then you shall roll it here that we may see it, when it is time to eat. It is a fried egg.

XVII

(AN INCANTATION)

Strung end to end are the precious stones, the red precious stones, representing the substance of heaven, the moisture of heaven.

The form in which you created the sun, in which you created the earth! The form of the moisture of heaven, the substance of heaven, the yellow blossom of heaven! How did I create your sun? How did I create your moon? How did I create your precious stones? I created you. When you were sprinkled with water, you remembered the force of the sun. Then when the message was sent to you ... Under cover I created you, I set you where you are . From time to time I take you , I perceive your vigor because of your father. You await ... that I may take away ... from your mouth. They are the yellow precious stones. So runs its course as he records it. These are the rulers which have been set in order. Go and read it and you will understand it.

XVIII

(A SERIES OF KATUN-PROPHECIES)

Katun 11 Ahau is established at Ichcaanzihoo. Yax-haal Chac is its face. The heavenly fan, the heavenly bouquet shall descend. The drum and rattle of Ah Bolon-yocte shall resound. At that time there shall be the green turkey; at that time there shall be Zulim Chan; at that time there shall be Chakanputun. They shall find their food among the trees; they shall find their food among the rocks, those who have lost their crops in Katun 11 Ahau.

The katun is established at Uuc-yab-nal in Katun 4 Ahau. At the mouth of the well, Uuc-yab-nal, it is established ... It shall dawn in the south. The face of the lord of the katun is covered; his face is dead. There is mourning for water; there is mourning for bread. His mat and his throne shall face the west. Blood-vomit is the charge of the katun . At that time his loin-cloth and his mantle shall be white. Unattainable shall be the bread of the katun. The quetzal shall come; the green bird shall come. The *kax* tree shall come; the bird shall come. The tapir shall come. The tribute shall be hidden at the mouth of the well.

The katun is established at Maylu, Zaci, Mayapan in Katun 2 Ahau. The katun stone is on its own base. The rope shall descend; the poison of the serpent shall descend, pestilence and three piles of skulls. The men are of little use. Then the burden was bound on Buluc-chabtan. Then there came up a dry wind. The ramon is the bread of Katun 2 Ahau. It shall be half famine and half abundance. This is the charge of Katun 2 Ahau.

The Katun is established at Kinchil Coba, Maya Cuzamil, in Katun 13 Ahau. Itzamna, Itzam-tzab, is his face during its reign. The ramon shall be eaten. Three years shall be locust years, ten generations of locusts . The fan shall be displayed; the bouquet shall be displayed, borne by Yaxaal Chac in the heavens. Unattainable is the bread of the katun in 13 Ahau. The sun shall be eclipsed. Double is the charge of the katun: men without offspring, chiefs without successors. For five days the sun shall be eclipsed, then it shall be seen again . This is the charge of Katun 13 Ahau.

XIX

(THE FIRST CHRONICLE)

A record of the count of the katuns since the discovery of Chichen Itzá occurred. It is written for the town in order that it may be known by anyone who wishes to be informed of the count of the katuns.

6 Ahau was when the discovery of Chichen Itzá occurred.

4 Ahau.

2 Ahau.

13 Ahau was when the mat of the katun was counted in order.

11 Ahau.

9 Ahau.

7 Ahau.

5 Ahau.

3 Ahau.

1 Ahau.

12 Ahau.

10 Ahau.

8 Ahau was when Chichen Itzá was abandoned. There were thirteen folds of katuns when they established their houses at Chakanputun.

6 Ahau.

4 Ahau was when the land was seized by them at Chakanputun.

2 Ahau.

13 Ahau.

11 Ahau.

9 Ahau.

7 Ahau.

5 Ahau.

3 Ahau.

1 Ahau.

12 Ahau.

10 Ahau.

8 Ahau was when Chakanputun was abandoned by the Itzá men. Then they came to seek homes again. For thirteen folds of katuns had they dwelt in their houses at Chakanputun. This was always the katun when the Itzá went beneath the trees, beneath the bushes, beneath the vines, to their misfortune.

6 Ahau.

4 Ahau.

2 Ahau.

13 Ahau.

11 Ahau.

9 Ahau.

7 Ahau.

5 Ahau.

3 Ahau.

1 Ahau.

12 Ahau.

10 Ahau.

8 Ahau was when the Itzá men again abandoned their homes because of the treachery of Hunac Ceel, because of the banquet with the people of Izamal. For thirteen folds of katuns they had dwelt there, when they were driven out by Hunac Ceel because of the giving of the questionnaire of the Itzá.

6 Ahau.

4 Ahau was when the land of Ich-paa Mayapan was seized by the Itzá men who had been separated from their homes because of the people of Izamal and because of the treachery of Hunac Ceel.

2 Ahau.

13 Ahau.

11 Ahau.

9 Ahau.

7 Ahau.

5 Ahau.

3 Ahau.

1 Ahau.

12 Ahau.

10 Ahau.

8 Ahau was when there was fighting with stones at Ich-paa Mayapan because of the seizure of the fortress. They broke down the city wall because of the joint government in the city of Mayapan.

6 Ahau.

4 Ahau was when the pestilence occurred; it was when the vultures entered the houses within the fortress.

2 Ahau was when the eruption of pustules occurred. It was smallpox.

13 Ahau was when the rain-bringer died. It was the sixth year. The year-count was to the east. It was the year 4 Kan. Pop was set to the east. . . . It was the fif teenth day of the month Zi mix was the day when the rain-bringer, Napot Xiu, died. It was the year of our Lord 158.

11 Ahau was when the mighty men arrived from the East. They were the ones who first brought disease here to our land, the land of us who are Maya, in the year 1513.

9 Ahau was when Christianity began, when baptism occurred. It was in this katun that Bishop Toral arrived here also. It was when the hangings ceased in the year of our Lord 1546.

7 Ahau was when Bishop de Landa died.

5 Ahau.

3 Ahau.

XX

(THE SECOND CHRONICLE)

4 Ahau was the name of the katun when occurred the birth of Pauahs, when the rulers descended.

Thirteen katuns they reigned; thus they were named while they ruled.

4 Ahau was the name of the katun when they descended; the great descent and the little descent they were called.

Thirteen katuns they reigned. So they were called. While they were settled, thirteen were their settlements.

4 Ahau was the katun when they sought and discovered Chichen Itzá. There it was that miraculous things were performed for them by their lords. Four divisions they were, when the four divisions of the nation, as they were called, went forth. From Kincolahpeten in the east one division went forth. From Nacocob in the north one division came forth. But one division came forth from Holtun Zuyua in the west. One division came forth from Four-peaked Mountain, Nine Mountains is the name of the land.

4 Ahau was the katun when the four divisions were called together . The four divisions of the nation, they were called, when they descended. They became lords when they descended upon Chichen Itzá. The Itzá were they then called.

Thirteen katuns they ruled, and then came the treachery by Hunac Ceel. Their town was abandoned and they went into the heart of the forest to Tan-xuluc-mul, as it is called.

4 Ahau was the katun when their souls cried out!

Thirteen katuns they ruled in their misery!

8 Ahau was the katun when occurred the arrival of the remainder of the Itzá, as they were called. They arrived, and there their reign endured in Chakanputun.

13 Ahau was the katun when they founded the town of Mayapan, the Maya men, as they were called.

8 Ahau was when their town was abandoned and they were scattered throughout the entire district. In the sixth katun after they were dispersed, then they ceased to be called Maya.

11 Ahau was the name of the katun when the Maya men ceased to be called Maya. They were called Christians; their entire province became subject to St. Peter and the reigning King of Spain .

XXI

(THE THIRD CHRONICLE)

A record of the katuns for the Itzá, called the Maya katuns.

12 Ahau.

10 Ahau.

8 Ahau.

6 Ahau was when the people of Conil were dispersed.

4 Ahau.

2 Ahau.

13 Ahau.

11 Ahau.

9 Ahau.

7 Ahau.

5 Ahau was when the town of the ruler of Izamal, Kinich Kakmoo as well as Pop-hol Chan was destroyed by Hunac Ceel.

3 Ahau.

1 Ahau was when the remainder of the Itzá were driven out of Chichen. It was the third tun of Katun 1 Ahau when Chichen was depopulated.

12 Ahau.

10 Ahau.

8 Ahau was the katun when the remainder of the Itzá founded their town, coming forth from beneath the trees and bushes at Tan-Xuluc-Mul, as it was called. They came out and established the land of Zaclactun Mayapan, as it was called. In the seventh tun of Katun 8 Ahau, this was the katun when Chakanputun perished at the hands of Kak-u-pacal and Tee Uilu.

6 Ahau.

4 Ahau.

2 Ahau.

13 Ahau.

11 Ahau.

9 Ahau.

7 Ahau.

5 Ahau was when foreigners arrived to eat men.

They were called foreigners without skirts. The land was not depopulated by them.

3 Ahau.

1 Ahau was when the district of Tancah Mayapan, as it was called, was depopulated. It was in the first tun of Katun 1 Ahau that the head-chief Tutul Xiu departed with the chiefs of the town and the four divisions of the town. This was the katun when the men of Tancah were dispersed and the chiefs of the town were scattered.

12 Ahau. The stone was taken at Otzmal.

10 Ahau. The stone was taken at Zizal.

8 Ahau. The stone was taken at Kancaba.

6 Ahau. The stone was taken at Hunacthi.

4 Ahau. The stone was taken at Atikuh. This was the katun when the pestilence occurred. It was in the fifth tun of Katun 4 Ahau.

2 Ahau. The stone was taken at Chacalna.

13 Ahau. The stone was taken at Euan.

11 Ahau. On the first day the stone was taken at Colox-peten.

This was the katun when the rain-bringer died; his name was Napot Xiu. It was in the first tun of 11 Ahau, that was the katun, when the

Spaniards first arrived here in our land. It was in the seventh tun of Katun 11 Ahau that Christianity then began; it was in the year A. D. 15 19.

9 Ahau. No stone was taken. This was the katun when Bishop Francisco Toral first arrived. He arrived in the sixth tun of Katun 9 Ahau.

7 Ahau. No stone was taken. This was the katun when Bishop de Landa died. Then another bishop also arrived.

5 Ahau.

3 Ahau.

On this 18th day of August, 1766, occurred a hurricane. I have made a record of it in order that it may be seen how many years it will be before another one will occur.

On this 20th day of January, 1782, there was an epidemic of inflammation here in the town of Chumayel. The swelling began at the neck and then descended. It spread from the little ones to the adults, until it swept the entire house, once it was introduced. The remedy was sour ashes and lemons or the young *Siempre vive*. It was the year of '81 when it began. After that there was a great drought also. There was scarcely any rain. The entire forest was burned with the heat , and the forest trees died This is the record which I have written down, I, Don Juan Josef Hoil. (Rubrica.)

Chumayel, June 28th, 1858, was when I made a loan to Chinuh Balam. I, Pedro Briceño. (Rubrica.)

XXII

(A BOOK OF KATUN-PROPHECIES)

Today, Wednesday, April 4th, 1832, I have recorded the name of Maria Isidora, daughter of Andres Balam and Maria Juana Xicum.

Today, Sunday, December 22d, 1833, I have recorded the name of Tomas, son of Andres Balam and Maria Xicum. God-father: José Maria Castañeda. God-mother: Manuela Marin.

Cura

. . . Justo Balam, Secretary. (Rubrica)

This is the day on which I purchased the book: July 1st, 1838. It cost me one peso in my poverty. This was the price I paid to the Señor Padre: one peso. This is the year of the purchase ... I have recorded it in order that it might be known that at this time it passed into my hands by purchase.

I, Pedro de Alcantara Briceño, resident of San Antonio.

(2. Historical introduction to the katun-prophecies.)

In Katun 13 Ahau the ship of the foreigners first appeared at Campeche. 1541 was the name of the year when they brought the news that the Maya men were to enter into Christianity, when the land of Tantun Cuzamil was established. They were there for half a year. Then they went to the seaport to the west and the people of Chikin-Chel were put under tribute. It was the year 1542 when the district of Tihoo, Ichcanziho, was established, in Katun 11 Ahau. The first governor was the Adelantado Don Francisco Montejo who was to appoint subjects for the foreigners, mighty men. In the year 1542 tribute was introduced. A. D. 1545 was the year when the Padres arrived, four years after the arrival of the foreigners. Then it was that men were baptised from town to town by the Padres . When they first arrived the towns were distributed among them.

1544 was the year . . . six hundred years and seventy-five years after the town of Chichen Itzá was depopulated, after its settlements were depopulated. It was eight hundred years and seventy years after the town of Uxmal was depopulated, after the people were driven out of its towns.

In the year 1537, on a day named 9 Cauac, was when the nobles gathered at the town of Mani to discuss fully whether they should go and bring the foreigners to their settlements because the head-chief had been killed. These were their names: Ah Moochan Xiu, Nahau Ez, Ah ¢un Chinab, Napoot Cupul, Napot Che, Nabatun Itza, Ah-kin Euan from Caucel, Nachan Uc from ¢ibilkal Ah-kin Ucan from Ekob, Nachi Uc, Ah-kul Koh, Nachan Motul, Nahau Coyi. These were the men of importance who talked of bringing the foreigners to their town, because the head-chief of the town, Ah ¢un Xiu was killed at Otzmal.

10 Kan was the year-bearer when the seeker for a town passed. He was called Montejo, he who wrote down the towns. This was the year when the strangers in the land, the foreigners who ate annonas, passed. They were the first to distribute the towns. It was when the foreigners arrived that the "receivers" received them. When they assembled at Campeche, when their ships came forth, then the nobles went to give gifts to them. There were thirteen "receivers of the foreigners." After that they came to Ichcanziho. 9 Ahau was the katun.

✠ This is a record of the wisdom of the book in which is set down the course of the katun. Here it is published in the land of Nitunȼala, Chactemal, Tahuaymil, Holtun Itzá, Chichinila, in order that the charge of the course of the katun may be known, of each katun, whether it is good or bad. Thus it is written by the Holy Writer, the Evangelist, it is the word of the Lord of heaven and earth . . . it comes from on high. This was given to them ... at the beginning of the land, at the beginning of our humanity ... the true word in Holy Writ, in the book, the *Reportorio*. It has no error; the seal on the book was carefully surveyed by them. These were the four lineages from heaven, the substance of heaven, the moisture of heaven, the head-chiefs, the rulers of the land: Zacaal Puc, Hooltun Balam, Hochtun Poot, Ah Mex-Cue Chan.

Behold, within seven score years Christianity will be introduced amid the clamor of the rulers, those who violently seize land during the katun. Then suddenly appears the wise man; then there is the examination of the katun. Miserable is the face of Chac Chuen Coyi. Then the Lord of the Church shall come. It is in the middle of the town of Tihoo. It shall come from the East, from the North, from the West, from the South; the word of Christianity shall be heard in the 17th tun in order that Christianity may truly arise.

The Padres shall arrive; the Bishop shall arrive, the Holy Inquisition, the word of God. These things shall be accomplished. No one shall cause them to cease. Amen.

(3. The katun-prophecies.)

The Chapter of the year, the katun.

First: 11 Ahau, when the foreigners first established the country.

The first: Katun 11 Ahau was the beginning of the katun-count, the first katun. The katun was established at Ichcaanzihoo when the foreigners arrived. Red were the beards of the children of the sun, the bearded ones from the east, when they arrived here in our land. The strangers to the land are white men, red men, . . . a beginning of carnal sin . . . Oh Itzá! . . . make ready. There cometh a white circle in the sky, the fair-skinned boy from

FIG. 30--The lord of the katun. (Chumayel MS.).

heaven, the white wooden standard that shall descend from heaven. A quarter of a league, a league away, it approaches. You shall see the dawn of a new day, you shall see the *mut*-bird. Oh! how there shall be intercession for us when they come. There shall come multitudes who gather stone and wood, the worthless rabble of the town. Fire shall flame up at the tips of their hands. There shall be sufficient poison and also ropes to hang their lords. Oh Itzá! Your worship is of no avail with the true God who has descended. It is false in word and teaching. Niggard is the katun; scanty are its rains. Who would be the priest, who would be the prophet who would understand it when he came to Tancah Mayapan or to Chichen Itzá? Alas! The burden laid upon the younger brothers; it came in Katun 7 Ahau through necessity, through misery, from the tribute, from the time it was first imposed upon you down to the tribute which you shall bear tomorrow and day after tomorrow in your children's time. Prepare yourselves to endure the burden of misery which is to come among your villages. This katun which has been established is, a katun of misery, a katun of the importunity of the devil, when it is established in Katun 11 Ahau. Receive your guests, the bearded men, the bearers of the sign of God. Your elder brothers, the men of Tantun, come. They shall ask of you an offering to God with them. Their priest was named Ah Miznilacpe. Their faces were like the puma, like Antichrist, on that day which is to come, on that day which confronts you, alas, in much misery, my sons. This is the word of our Lord: "It shall burn on earth, there shall be a white circle in the sky, in that katun in time to come." It is the true word from the mouth of God the Father. Alas, very heavy is the burden of the katun that shall be established in Christianity. When it comes there shall be slavish talk, slavish ... servile men. When it comes, there shall be . . . you shall see. There shall come the head-chiefs ... the two day occupants of the thrones and mats ... in the five unlucky days at the end of the year, in the days of penance. This only is the end of the word of God. 11 is the cup of the katun . The news regarding the aspect of its reign is gathered, all its teachings, all its words. You shall die; you shall live; but you may not understand the word of the living book. Ah Maypan was his only son, his justice. He was put in prison, he was taken out, then he was bound and whipped. After that, when he was seated, the son was admonished. There was a hat on his head and sandals on his feet. A cord was tied about his waist when he came.

The second katun .

Katun 9 Ahau is the second katun of the count. The katun was established at Ichcaanzihoo. Then it was that the foreigners to the land received their tribute. Then it was that the fathers of our souls arrived. The scattered

divisions of the towns under their local chieftains were gathered together. They began to teach the holy faith and baptise us. The foundations of the holy Cathedral were laid, the public house of God, the widely extended house of God the Father. Then the seven sacraments were established to take away our sins . . . There began to be much labor in the center of the town . . . the misery of the world. Then there was set up . . . the word of God, which shall also come from the mouth of God the Father. Then the fair complexioned boy arrives, he comes from heaven. The Virgin, as she is called, is the mother of the seven planets.

It was in the ninth year of Katun 9 Ahau that they served Christianity, just as it was written by the prophet Chilam Balam on the stone of nine seals in heaven. 13 E¢nab was the day there in heaven as well as here on earth. There was the heavenly staff, the heavenly fan. The cord descended, the word of God which came from on high all over the entire world. Nine was its plate, nine was its cup. Oh make ready, Itzá. Nowhere shall you offer provocation to your guests. You shall give them food to eat, and they shall also give you food to eat when they come.

The third katun .

p. 90 C

Katun 7 Ahau is the third katun. The katun is established at Ichcaanzihoo. Yaxal Chac is the face of the katun in the heavens to its ruler, to its wise man, while the drum resounds below and the rattle resounds above. The Plumeria is its bread, the Plumeria is its water, the burden of the katun . Then begins the lewdness of the wise men, the beckoning of carnal sin, the beckoning of the katun. The katun begins to limp; it is all over the world. Carnal sin is its garment, carnal sin is its face, carnal sin is its ... carnal sin is its sandal, carnal sin is its head, carnal sin is its gait. They twist their necks, they twist their mouths, they wink the eye, they slaver at the mouth, at men, women, chiefs, justices, presiding officers, clerks, choir-masters, everybody both great and small. There is no great teaching. Heaven and earth are truly lost to them; they have lost all shame. Then the head-chiefs of the towns, the rulers of the towns, the prophets of the towns, the priests of the Maya men are hanged. Understanding is lost; wisdom is lost. Prepare yourselves, oh Itzá! Your sons shall see the mirth of the katun, the jesting of the katun. Dissolute is the speech, dissolute the face of the rogue to the rulers, to the head-chiefs. Seven is the plate, seven the cup of the katun , it is the word of God. Much hanging of men is the charge of the katun.

The fourth katun .

Katun 5 Ahau is the fourth katun. The katun is established at Ichcaanzihoo. Harsh is its face, harsh its tidings, to the ruler. There is affliction of the offspring of woman and man, when it comes. Then begins the vexation by the devil in the world. Then came the blinding of the face of the god , the face of Kauil, in the four changing heavens, the four changing roads. Then hanging comes to the world. The red rattlesnake raises its head to bite; the *holil- och* raises its head to bite . Men and women have few children. Then came ... the end of the cigar, after the lord of the world was created ... he heard the dance. . . There is the red flowered thing, the red *xulab*, the red *uayah-cab*, the accessory of the rattle of the giver of our hearts in tribute through misery and vexation. It is the opossum chieftain, the fox chieftain, the *ah-pic* chieftain, the blood- sucking chieftain, the avaricious ones of the town. He is set up perchance, and then it is that your drum is beaten, my younger brother my elder brother. He who lies in wait for you on all fours is among you, the *tolil-och*. It is his katun. The Plumeria flower is his chair, as he sits on his throne. He is publicly seen in the market-place on his mat, the two-day occupant of the throne, the two-day occupant of the mat.

They deceive the town, the two town officials, the chieftain opossum and he who lies in wait on all fours. They bring the pestilence, they are the cause of ...; there was little of it formerly. You then called them the Itzá. The rattle of the katun is shaken; there is the treachery of the katun at Tancah Mayapan. There is the great tribute of Zuyua. The kinkajou claws the back of the jaguar amid the affliction of the katun, amid the affliction of the year; they are greedy for dominion. Many hangings are the charge of the katun, when the chiefs of the town are hung there. There is an end to the misery of the Maya men when suddenly the men of Uaymil come to take vengeance on the world.

The fifth katun. 1620.

Katun 3 Ahau was the fifth katun. The katun was established at Ichcaanzihoo. Ek-Cocah-mut was its face to the rulers, to the wise men. Antichrist was its face to the rulers. Fire shall flame up at the horn of the brockett at Ichcaanzihoo. The skin of the jaguar shall be spread out in the marketplace. The water-tank is its tidings. There are rains of little profit, rains from a rabbit sky, rains from a parched sky, rains from a woodpecker sky, high rains, rains from a vulture sky, crested rains, deer rains. Then descends the thrice raised leaf of the *zil*-palm. There is fighting; there is a year of locusts. The diminished remainder of the population is hanged. They are defeated in war. Sad shall be the havoc at the cross-roads. There are the lords of the army; their souls cry out at the opening up of the town ...

Behold, I am Katun 3 Ahau. My town of Ichcaanzihoo is founded. Behold, I am Caesar Augustus. . . . I receive my donation in the heart of the forest

The first katun .

Katun 1 Ahau is the seventh katun. The katun is established at Emal. At that time Ix Puc-yola and Ox Ualacii shall come. The rope shall descend, the cord shall descend. There comes from heaven the word of the true path. Through it will come the fulfilment of the word of the Lord of heaven, the true word.

The dog is its tidings; the vulture is its tidings. The flag is the second of the figures drawn above . The opossum is its face to the rulers. Thrice impeded are their thought and speech, thrice impeded their manhood, thrice impeded their flint knife among the rulers, among the wise men. Then came Hunpic-ti-ax as an affliction, the jaguar and Canul for an affliction. These were the eaters of their food, the destroyers of their crops, the *boboch*, the destroyer of food. For seven years there is the affliction of Hunpic-ti-ax; for seven years there is the affliction of Canul. Then the justice of our Lord, God, shall descend upon carnal sin, upon the worthless rabble of the town, upon the lewd rogue, the rascal. After that there shall come another word, another teaching, but the Maya men shall not admit it to their hearts. The word of God, the Father of Heaven, shall be sung among them that they may correct their ways, that they may turn their backs upon their evil ways, the usages among Maya men; but they will not wish to listen to the word of God, when they should rather respect the judges as their fathers. The hearts of the head-chiefs of the world shall be sad. They believe little, nor do they even believe that. So you say. The blessed among those in authority are set apart. Fire shall be kindled with a fire-drill as a sign of the Maya Virgin. Hunab-ku is in his only virgin Church, where he cries out. There is heard the word of the Lord of Heaven, the Lord on earth. The entire world shall be sad when he comes. The wing of the land shall shake, the center of the land shall shake when he comes in his time. Then there shall occur the obedience of the foreigners of Bentana to the word of God. Thrice shall the justice of our Lord descend to the world. Then a great army shall descend upon the worthless rabble of the town, that it may be known whether their faith is truly firm. Then descended the governor. There shall begin the tearing out of the eyes: of the rogue who incites riot, of the great rascal, of the great hawk of the town, of the fox of the town. Then the eternal ruler shall come to cut the cord from the burden of misery, the ruler who appraises. Then sickness, the result of guilt, shall descend, the punishment of all the world shall come from heaven, with it the drought. At that time it shall be all over the world. The remainder of the guardians of the sands, the guardians of the sea, shall be detained together such as the people of Uaymil, such as the people of Emal. The rest of them shall be assembled in great numbers by the sea at the end of the katun. Thus it is seen that the fold of the katun is brought about. Then the flag shall be raised. Then there is an end to the importunity of the devil, of Antichrist. There is knife-thrusting strife, purse-snatching strife, strife with the blow-gun, strife by trampling on people, stonethrowing strife. The fighting ends in the heart of the forest where Cæsar Augustus receives his donation. There is sudden death with hunger; the vultures enter, the houses because of the pestilence. There is sad havoc with flies swarming at the cross-roads, and at the four resting places at the four corners . There is oppression of the younger brothers, flaying of the sons; it comes to the world. Then arrives the ruler to propound the riddle to them. His face is that of a war-captain, of the son of God. After that there is the arrival of the Bishop, the Holy Inquisition as it is called, and Saul. They ask for penitence and Christianity. There is an end to greed, an end to vexation in the world. This shall be the end of its prophecy: there is a great war. The Chan s shall rise up in war with the five divisions of Chakan, an army of Chan s in Katun I Ahau. A parching whirlwind storm is the charge of the katun. There is a series of rains, rain from a rabbit-sky during the evil katun. There is a sudden end to planting. Then the burden of legal summons descends; tribute descends; the proof is sought, with seven fathoms . . ., when the serving of God is strongly urged.

It is the end of receiving the money of Antichrist. Antichrist does not come, our Lord God does not desire it. The katun is not ruined here in our land by the natives of our land. This was the origin of Antichrist, it was avarice; but before the coming of the mighty men there was no robbery by violence, there was no greed and striking down one's fellow man in his blood, at the cost of the poor man, at the expense of the food of each and every one. In time to come there shall be five fruits of the tree for the food of the kinkajou, the man of Bentena. Alas, there is sorrow in the heart of the Lord of Heaven. Smallpox is the end of the prophecy of the katun. An army shall come forth from Havana with a fleet of thirteen ships.

The second katun .

Katun 12 Ahau is the eighth katun of the count. The katun is established at Zaclahtun. Yaxal Chuen is his face, Buleu-caan-chac is his face to the rulers. He shall manifest himself. He is in the sky by day; he is in the sky by night. The great artisan, the wise man shall come . There are kind head-chiefs, kind chiefs; kindness and joy is the law of the entire world. Poor men become rich. Abundance of bread is the word of the katun. It is a rich year; there is an accumulation of wealth also. The katun is good. The rains are good ones; the fruit will form. Then they come forth from among the rocks to Christianity, where God is. There shall be neither the fox nor the kinkajou that will bite. Then penitence is sought of the town officials, with the opening of the golden gates and the town marriages in the official building. Then our

sandals are sought for, in the time of our Christianity. This is a new day which dawns for us; this is what you tell of today. This shall be the end of the katun of carnal sin. Soon shall it end. The law of the ruler comes. Then there shall come the Seven Mountains, the Red Star, and in the wind-swollen sky there shall be the House of Storms, in the 17th tun.

The third katun .

Katun 10 Ahau, the katun is established at Chable. The ladder is set up over the rulers of the land. The hoof shall burn; the sand by the seashore shall burn; the bird's nest shall burn. The rocks shall crack with the heat ; drought is the charge of the katun. It is the word of our Lord God the Father and of the Mistress of Heaven, the portent of the katun.

No one shall arrest the word of our Lord God, God the Son, the Lord of Heaven and earth. There shall not be lacking that which shall, through his power, come to pass all over the world. Holy Christianity shall come bringing with it the time when the stupid ones who speak our language badly shall turn from their evil ways. No one shall prevent it; this then is the drought. Sufficient is the word for the Maya priests, the word of God.

8 Ahau is the next fold, the fourth katun .

The fourth katun .

Katun 8 Ahau is the ninth katun. The katun is established at Izamal. There is Kinich Kakmo. The shield shall descend, the arrow shall descend upon Chakanputun together with the rulers of the land. The heads of the foreigners to the land were cemented into the wall at Chakanputun. There is an end of greed; there is an end to causing vexation in the world. It is the word of God the Father. Much fighting shall be done by the natives of the land.

The fifth katun .

Katun 6 Ahau is the tenth katun according to the count. The katun is established at Uxmal. The katun monuments are set up on their own bases. Shameless is his speech, shameless his face to the rulers. They shall be the inventors of lewd speech, and then God the Father shall descend to cut their throats because of their sins. Then they shall be regenerated; the judgment of our Lord God shall unite them until they enter into Christianity with their families. As many as are born here on earth shall enter into Christianity.

The first katun .

Katun 4 Ahau is the eleventh katun according to the count. The katun is established at Chichen Itzá. The settlement of the Itzá shall take place there . The quetzal shall come, the green bird shall come. Ah Kantenal shall come. Blood-vomit shall come. Kukulcan shall come with them for the second time. It is the word of God. The Itzá shall come.

The second katun .

Katun 2 Ahau is the twelfth katun. At Maya Cuzamil the katun is established. For half the katun there will be bread; for half the katun there will be water. It is the word of God. For half of it there will be a temple for the rulers. It is the end of the word of God.

The third katun .

The judgment.

83

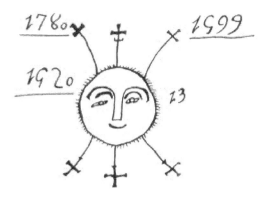

It is Katun 13 Ahau according to the count. The katun is established at Kinchil Coba, the thirteenth katun. The bouquet of the rulers of the world shall be displayed. There is the universal judgment of our Lord God. Blood shall descend from the tree and stone. Heaven and earth shall burn. It is the word of God the Father, God the Son and God the Holy Spirit. It is the holy judgment, the holy judgment of our Lord God. There shall be no strength in heaven and earth. Great cities shall enter into Christianity, any settlements of people whatever, the great towns, whatever their names are as well as the little towns, all over our land of Maya Cuzamil Mayapan. It shall be for our two-day men, because of lewdness . . . the sons of malevolence. At the end of our blindness and shame our sons shall be regenerated from carnal sin. There is no lucky day for us. It is the cause of death from bad blood, when the moon rises, when the moon sets, the entire moon, this was its power; it was all blood. So it was with the good planets which were looked upon as good. It is the end of the word of God. The waters of baptism shall come over them, the Holy Spirit. They receive the holy oil without compulsion; it comes from God. There are too many Christians who go to those who deny the holy faith, . . . to the Itzá and the *balams*. There is then an end to our losing

XXIII

(THE LAST JUDGMENT)

The judgment of God for the righteous: "Come unto me ye blessed of my Father, inherit the eternal glory prepared by my Father for you since the beginning of the world. You have kept my commandments; you have done penance when you sinned against me. Therefore come ye to heaven." Then he turns his gaze upon the sinners with whom he is angered. "Depart from me ye accursed of my Father into the eternal fire of hell which is prepared for the Devil by my Father. You have despised me, your Father, me, your Redeemer. You have despised my commandments with the commandment of the Devil. Go ye therefore with him to eternal misery." Then the wicked men shall go to hell, but the good men shall go to Heaven with our Father, God, to eternal glory comparable to the glory of Jehoshaphat. There are three men, the true servants of God, well beloved of God. Elias, and Methuselah and Enoch are their names; they are living to this day. They are ordained by God to guard his seats. Our Lord God shall call a reckoning in a valley in the land, a great open savannah. There he shall sit upon his throne. The entire world shall assemble there . The sheep shall be set apart; they shall be on his right hand. The goats shall be set apart; they shall be on his left hand. On his left shall be the wicked men; those who have not fulfilled all the commandments of God shall then go to the eternal misery of hell, sunk in the earth, oppressed by the Sins of our first parents. But the good men who have fulfilled the commandments of God shall be at the right hand of the great Lord God. "Come, ye men blessed of my Father and take the kingdom prepared for you since the beginning of the world." Then a great cloud shall gather, black in the sky, down to the face of the earth. Like a trumpet is the joyful song of the Angels. It is beautiful beyond comparison. The true God shall arise, the Lord of heaven and earth.

XXIV

(PROPHECIES OF A NEW RELIGION)

These are the words which were composed to admonish the fatherless ones, the motherless ones. These words are to be treasured as a precious jewel is treasured. They are concerning the coming introduction of Christianity, and were spoken at Tancah Mayapan and at Chichen Itzá in the time of the Zuyua people, in the time of the Itzá. A new wisdom shall dawn upon the world universally, in the east, north, west and south. It shall come from the mouth of God the Father. Those who recorded it were the five priests, the holy priests who came into the presence of God. They recorded the charge of misfortune when the introduction of Christianity came.

Here are their names written down:

1. Chilam Balam, the great priest.

2. Napuctun, the great priest.

3. Nahau Pech, the great priest.

4. Ah Kuil Chel, the great priest.

5. Natzin Yabun Chan, the great priest.

Like a servant of God who bends his back over virgin soil, they recorded the charge of misery in the presence of our Lord God: the introduction of Christianity occurs; blood-vomit, pestilence, drought, a year of locusts, smallpox are the charge of misery, also the importunity of the devil. There shall be a white circle in the sky. It shall burn on earth in Katun 3

Ahau, in Katun 1 Ahau, the worst of three katuns. Just as it was written by the Evangelists and the prophet Balam, it came from the mouth of the Lord of heaven and earth. Then the priests set it down in holy writ at the time of the great drought at Lahun Chable in the time of Christianity. Then Saul and Don Antonio Martínez shall come to avenge their descendants. The day has dawned. So it is written in the command of the great priest, the prophet of Chilam Balam and in the chest of manuscripts. Amen Jesus.

The Interpretation of the histories of Yucatan.

The priests, the prophecy of Napuctun.

It shall burn on earth; there shall be a circle in the sky. Kauil shall be set up; he shall be set up in front in time to come. It shall burn on earth; the very hoof shall burn in that katun, in the time which is to come. Fortunate is he who shall see it when the prophecy is declared, who shall weep over his misfortunes in time to come.

The prophecy of Ah Kuil Chel, the priest.

When the end of the katun shall come, lord, ye shall not understand when it comes. Who shall believe it at the rolling up of the mat of the katun? The end shall come because of misery. It comes from the north, it comes from the west at that time when it shall be, lord. Who then shall be the priest, who then shall be the prophet who will declare truly the word of the book, lord, in Katun 9 Ahau? Ye shall not understand, ye people in every part of the world . . . shall be cleansed of shame. Oh there was joy among the rulers, pleasure among the rulers of the land. Acknowledge it in your hearts, ye Itzá.

The prophecy of Nahau Pech the great priest.

At that time when the sun shall stand high in the heavens , lord, when the ruler has had compassion, in the fourth katun it shall come to pass, the tidings of God are truly brought. They ask perchance what I recommend, lord. You see your guests upon the road, oh Itzá! It is the fathers of the land who will arrive. This prophecy comes from the mouth of Nahau Pech, the priest in the time of Katun 4 Ahau at the end of the katun, lord.

The food of the ant -like men shall be destroyed. They shall be at the end of their food -supply because of the *boboch* which takes their food, the great hawk which takes their food, the ant, the cowbird, the grackle, the blackbird, the mouse.

The prophecy of Natzin Yabun Chan.

There was the word of the true God in the land. You shall await the coming forth, lord, of his priests who will bring it in time to come. Give your understanding to his word, to his admonition. Fortunate are you who truly receive it. Forsake those things which you have held sacred, oh Itzá; forget your perishable gods, your transitory gods. Of all things he is the ruler, lord, the creator of all heaven and earth. It is to your hearts that I speak, oh Maya Itzá. You shall not desire another God than the true God according to your own words. You shall take to heart the word of my admonition.

The prophecy of Chilam Balam, the singer, of Cabal-chen, Mani.

On the day 13 Ahau the katun will end in the time of the Itzá, in the time of

Tancah Mayapan , lord. There is the sign of Hunab-ku on high. The raised wooden standard shall come. It shall be displayed to the world, that the world may be enlightened, lord. There has been a beginning of strife, there has been a beginning of rivalry, when the priestly man shall come to bring the sign of God in time to come, lord. A quarter of a league, a league away he comes. You see the *mut* -bird surmounting the raised wooden standard. A new day shall dawn in the north, in the west.

Itzamná Kauil shall rise. Our lord comes, Itzá. Our elder brother comes, oh men of Tantun. Receive your guests, the bearded men, the men of the east, the bearers of the sign of God, lord. Good indeed is the word of God that comes to us. The day of our regeneration comes. You do not fear the world, Lord, you are the only God who created us. It is sufficient, then, that the word of God is good, lord. He is the guardian of our souls. He who receives him, who has truly believed, he will go to heaven with him. Nevertheless at the beginning were the two-day men.

Let us exalt his sign on high, let us exalt it that we may gaze upon it today with the raised standard. Great is the discord that arises today. The First Tree of the World is restored; it is displayed to the world. This is the sign of Hunab-ku on high. Worship it, Itzá. You shall worship today his sign on high. You shall worship it furthermore with true good will, and you shall worship the true God today, lord. You shall be converted to the word of Hunab-ku, lord; it came from heaven. Oh it is he who speaks to you! Be admonished indeed, Itzá. They will correct their ways who receive him in their hearts in another katun, lord.

Believe in my word itself, I am Chilam Balam, and I have interpreted the entire message of the true God of the world; it is heard in every part of the world, lord, the word of God, the Lord of heaven and earth. Very good indeed is his word in heaven, lord.

He is ruler over us; he is the true God over our souls.

But those to whom the word is brought, lord: thrice weighed down is their strength, the younger brothers native to the land. Their hearts are submerged in sin . Their hearts are dead in their carnal sins. They are frequent backsliders, the principal ones who spread sin , Nacxit Xuchit in the carnal sin of his companions, the two-day rulers. They sit crookedly on their thrones; crookedly in carnal sin. Two-day men they call them. For two days endure their seats, their cups, their hats. They are the unrestrained lewd ones of the day, the unrestrained lewd ones of the night, the rogues of the world. They twist their necks, they wink their eyes, they slaver at the mouth, at the rulers of the land, lord. Behold, when they come, there is no truth in the words of the foreigners to the land. They tell very solemn and mysterious things, the sons of the men of Seven-deserted-buildings, the offspring of the women of Seven-deserted-buildings, lord.

Who will be the prophet, who will be the priest who shall interpret truly the word of the book?